TALES OF THE DEAD

A ZOMBIE ANTHOLOGY

OTHER LIVING DEAD PRESS BOOKS

PLANET OF THE DEAD: BOOKS 1 & 2
NOVELLAS OF THE DEAD
TALES OF THE DEAD: A ZOMBIE ANTHOLOGY
ONLY THE YOUNG SURVIVE: AN APOCALYPTIC TALE
TALES OF BIGFOOT ANTHOLOGY
CLAN OF THE BIGFOOT * ZOMBIES AND POWER TOOLS
THE TURNING: A STORY OF THE LIVING DEAD * MEN OF PERDITION
THE DEAD OF SPACE BOOK 1 AND 2 * THE BABYLONIAN CURSE
PLAYING GOD: A ZOMBIE NOVEL * THE JUNKYARD
THE HAUNTED THEATRE
ZOMBIES IN OUR HOMETOWN
NIGHT OF THE WOLF: A WEREWOLF ANTHOLOGY
JUST BEFORE NIGHT: A ZOMBIE ANTHOLOGY
THE BOOK OF HORROR * KNIGHT SYNDROME
THE WAR AGAINST THEM: A ZOMBIE NOVEL
CHILDREN OF THE VOID * DARK DREAMS
BLOOD RAGE & DEAD RAGE (BOOK 1& 2 OF THE RAGE VIRUS SERIES)
DEAD MOURNING: A ZOMBIE HORROR STORY
BOOK OF THE DEAD: A ZOMBIE ANTHOLOGY VOLUME 1-6
LOVE IS DEAD: A ZOMBIE ANTHOLOGY
ETERNAL NIGHT: A VAMPIRE ANTHOLOGY
END OF DAYS: AN APOCALYPTIC ANTHOLOGY VOLUME 1-5
DEAD HOUSE: A ZOMBIE GHOST STORY
THE ZOMBIE IN THE BASEMENT
THE LAZARUS CULTURE: A ZOMBIE NOVEL
DEAD WORLDS: UNDEAD STORIES VOLUMES 1-7
FAMILY OF THE DEAD * REVOLUTION OF THE DEAD
KINGDOM OF THE DEAD * DEAD HISTORY
THE MONSTER UNDER THE BED * DEAD THINGS
DEAD TALES: SHORT STORIES TO DIE FOR
ROAD KILL: A ZOMBIE TALE * DEADFREEZE * DEADFALL
SOUL EATER * THE DARK * RISE OF THE DEAD
DEAD END: A ZOMBIE NOVEL * VISIONS OF THE DEAD
THE CHRONICLES OF JACK PRIMUS
INSIDE THE PERIMETER: SCAVENGERS OF THE DEAD
BOOK OF CANNIBALS VOLUME 2 * CHRISTMAS IS DEAD…AGAIN
EMAILS OF THE DEAD * CHILDREN OF THE DEAD
THE DEADWATER SERIES
DEADWATER * DEADWATER: Expanded Edition
DEADRAIN * DEADCITY * DEADWAVE * DEAD HARVEST
DEAD UNION * DEAD VALLEY * DEAD TOWN * DEAD GRAVE
DEAD SALVATION * DEAD ARMY (Book 10 Coming soon)

TALES OF THE DEAD

A ZOMBIE ANTHOLOGY

EDITED BY
ANTHONY GIANGREGORIO

TALES OF THE DEAD

Table of Contents

FOREWORD 1
POSTAGE DUE BY REBECCA SNOW 3
*THE DOG, THE DEAD MAN, THE POSTMAN AND HIS
LOVER* BY RICK MOORE 14
UNDEAD DELIVERY BY ANTHONY GIANGREGORIO 28
AUNT MAE'S FUNERAL BY J.L PETTY. 39
A NEW WORLD ORDER BY SUZANNE ROBB 43
HOW DO YOU EAT A WHOLE HUMAN? BY DANE T.
HATCHELL 62
TRAPPED BY P. A. DOUGLAS 73
BONE CLEANERS BY KATIE SIMMONS 83
POST OFFICE OF THE DEAD BY A. GIANGREGORIO 113
Z DAY BY AARON ALPER 131
ROUTE Z BY PATRICK MACADOO 140
THE FINAL PERFORMANCE BY MATT KURTZ 156
RAGE AGAINST THE DEAD BY DARREN WJ MILLS 160
YELLOW GOES TO YELOW, RED GOES TO RED BY KELLY
HUDSON 170
ABOUT THE WRITERS 183

FOREWORD

So here was this awesome picture of a zombie in the face of a scared mailman.

It was cover art that would work great for a zombie book. The only problem was that the picture was so special it couldn't be used on *any* old zombie book. Now the front could have been used by itself but that would have taken a lot away from its power, as it's really one full piece.

So here was a fun cover and no idea what it could be used for.

A few other small publishers had done artwork-inspired anthologies, one where the picture tells a story and then all the writer has to do is go with it.

So that's what happened here and what came of it is a great collection of really fun stories, thanks in no small part to the cover art of this book, which tells a story just by looking at it. They say a picture is worth a thousand words and in this case, they're correct and then some.

I mean, the cover art of this book simply screams for a back story, doesn't it? How did that zombie get there, what's going to happen to that little postman?

Will his letters ever get delivered? Will he become zombie chow?

So now you know where this anthology came from and as you read these stories, think of the cover art to this book, because that's where the inspiration for the tales within came from.

All I know is, when I look at the cover art of this book and see that imposing zombie about to take the letter carrier's head off, I know one thing, and one thing only.

I wouldn't want to be the mail carrier for that neighborhood.

Anthony Giangregorio
July 2011

POSTAGE DUE

REBECCA SNOW

Frank stepped onto the curb and hiked up his gray uniform pants. The mailbag strapped across his chest hugged him like a baby gorilla and hid his sunken chest from anyone who might find his perspiring face appealing. A small package rested in the bend of his arm as he lifted the bolt on the rusted, chain-link gate. The hinges shrieked but didn't bar entrance to the fenced yard. Distant thunder rumbled among the scattered clouds.

The clank of the closing latch echoed through the dense branches surrounding the property. Waist-high weeds muffled laughter from children down the street. A crow cawed a welcome before flapping from a high limb. Frank flinched but kept walking toward where he thought the house might be. He'd only delivered advertisements to this address, and even then, he'd deposited the flyers in the rusty receptacle at the head of the lane. He didn't know who removed the solicitations once a month, but like clockwork, every first Monday, he had an empty box to refill. He stared down at the smudged red ink. If it hadn't been for the missing two dollars in postage, he could have left the parcel with the other leaflets.

A cloudbank drifted over the sun as Frank turned a corner on the unkempt path. The dilapidated house loomed from the shadows. Ivy clung to the remaining pieces of intricate gingerbread trim, the few shutters still left hanging at odd angles. Jagged glass poked from broken, second story panes. Leprous paint peeled from the once white siding. A cat skittered across the warped porch boards and jumped into a scraggly hedgerow. Frank spun to glance back through the trees before he gripped the wobbling railing and placed his foot on the first step.

A howling creak preceded the crumbling of rotten wood. His foot punctured the tread, and he tumbled to the ground, still grasping the railing in his clammy hand. The package toppled end over end and came to rest against a moss-covered tree trunk. Frank released the railing with a grunt and rolled to his knees. The mail sack snagged on a tree root as he rose, letters fluttering from a fresh hole in the canvas sack. Lifting the straps over his head, he hurled the bag to the ground but stopped short of grinding the envelopes into the dirt with his shoe.

"Stupid package," he said. He reached down to retrieve the offending item and read the label. "I hope Dr. William Bower appreciates whatever's in this thing."

Pressing the packet to his ear, he gave the box a cursory shake. When something jingled behind the taped flaps, he scanned the yard to see if anyone else had heard.

Dead leaves fluttered to rest in front of the ancient door though Frank hadn't felt a breeze. He dusted himself off and stepped back onto the porch, avoiding the hole he'd made in the stair. The face of a tarnished lion stared with unblinking eyes from a brass knocker. He took a breath and tapped twice. After a moment, he repeated his rapping. Reaching into his back pocket, he pulled out a small yellow pad and a pen. As he began filling in the blanks on the **Sorry We Missed You** card, the door opened.

Frank looked up to see the grayest face he'd ever encountered, even grayer than the faces he'd seen when delivering mail to the mortuary on Tenth Street. Two cloudy eyes gazed at his hairline.

"P-p-postage due," Frank stammered. He lifted a hand to smother his cowlick. "Two dollars, please."

The sallow man opened his mouth and groaned. A whiff of putrid morning breath floated through the air, although it was at least an hour after noon. The postman stepped away from the stink and coughed.

"I understand the inconvenience, sir." Frank scratched the back of his neck with his free hand and sighed. "But I can't deliver this package until the postage is paid."

The customer shambled forward and fumbled with the mailman's collar. Swatting at the clutching fingers, Frank stumbled backwards, cornering himself between a porch column and a tree growing through the floorboards.

"Get off me," he said. "I'll call the cops."

The ashen-skinned man ignored Frank's plea and took another step toward him. Cringing into the tree trunk, Frank squeezed his eyes shut and waited for the first blow to fall.

"Edgar!" a voice called from the dark interior of the house. "Edgar, are you tormenting that poor man?"

Another shuffling step sounded on the hardwood as a frail, gray-haired man tottered into view. Frank ducked as Edgar swung a clawed hand at his face.

"Edgar!" the man said. "Stop that this minute, or so help me, I'll put you back in the grave where I found you!"

The reaching arms lowered as Edgar's chin dropped to his chest.

"That's better," the voice said in a calmer tone. "Now, step away from the nice man, so he can breathe."

Edgar hobbled to a corner of the porch without making eye contact with either of the men. Frank slid down the column and rested his arms on his knees.

"Thanks for the rescue." Frank waved a hand at Edgar. "What's wrong with that guy? All I wanted was the two dollars due on this package." He nudged the small cardboard box with his toe.

"Please accept my apologies," the older gentleman said, reaching out a furrowed hand. "I'm Dr. Bower, but you can call me Bill. Edgar is having a few problems adjusting to his reanimation."

Frank hesitated before accepting the man's outstretched, bony fingers. "His what?"

Dr. Bower grunted as he pulled the postman to his feet.

"His rising, his rebirth." He gasped, trying to catch his breath. "He's been dead for three weeks and undead for two days." Puffing out his cheeks, the old man exhaled for half a minute before continuing. "Considering his limited capabilities, I think he's doing remarkably well. Don't you?"

Frank stood with his mouth open in a position his mother would have called, 'catching flies.' His eyes flicked from Dr. Bower to Edgar before sliding back to rest again on the doctor.

"He can't be dead. He's walking. The dead don't walk." Frank stretched a hand toward the zombie. "How?"

"Please don't touch." Dr. Bower lifted his cane and jostled the postman's elbow. "He isn't fully trained."

"How can he be walking if he's dead?" Frank's arms hung limp at his sides with the package clutched in his trembling hand. Craning his neck, he tried to get a better look at the impossibility.

"It's a scientific process. You wouldn't understand." The old man pursed his lips and squinted beady eyes behind wire-framed glasses.

"Is he dangerous?" Frank asked, eyes widening.

Bill gave his head a quick shake and glanced at the deformed boards under his feet. "No, he's harmless. Unless you provoke him."

"But he attacked me," Frank said, pointing a quaking finger at Edgar's slouching form.

"You made a demand he didn't understand."

"I asked him for two dollars." Frank threw his arms in the air. "How provoking is that?"

Edgar stiffened. A groan rumbled in his chest, and he began to raise his right arm.

"Edgar, go inside." Dr. Bower moved away from the door, and the zombie shuffled through the opening and disappeared from sight. "Sir, I said he wasn't fully re-educated in the ways of the living. You'll have to excuse his lapse of judgment."

Frank lowered himself to the bottom step. "I don't think I can. What would that thing have done if you hadn't come out here?" A frightened smirk bloomed on his face. "Eaten my brains? Bitten my nose off?"

"He didn't harm you, did he?" Dr. Bower's wispy white eyebrows rose.

"Well, no," Frank said. "But that isn't what I asked. Would I be dead if you hadn't stopped him?"

"Of course not," the doctor snapped before clearing his throat. "You mentioned you had a package?"

Frank started at the man's tone. "Yeah, I need two dollars though."

The doctor dug in his cardigan's deep pockets and came up with a tissue, three cents, and a small wad of lint.

"I have the money inside. Would you like to come in out of the heat while I find my change purse?" Dr. Bower clutched the gnarled head of his walking stick. "I'm sure Edgar would like to apologize."

Glancing back at his abandoned mailbag, Frank wiped his forehead on his shirtsleeve. The thick air and darkening sky predicted a storm. The cool darkness beckoned him, but the thought of Edgar waiting in a shadowy corner made him reconsider.

"I think it's best if I wait here." He shoved the half-crumpled parcel under his arm and returned to his damaged mailbag. After a moment had passed, he looked up from the scattered mail to see that the doctor was gone.

Upon inspection, Frank found that the ragged tear in the mail sack made securing the mail impossible. He gathered up the envelopes and set the stack under the bag to prevent them from flying away in a wayward breeze. Brushing the dirt from his hands, he crept to the front door and peered into the unlit foyer.

"Hello?" he called. "Dr. Bower?" Frank listened to the ticking of an unseen clock. "Bill?"

A woman in a stained and tattered white gown stumbled from a hallway. She gurgled a guttural moan. A blood bubble burst from her lips. Her glazed eyes seemed to follow his voice.

"Doctor?" Frank called, panicking.

The figure reached for him, and turning to run, he collided with Edgar. A cloud of dust and live moths exploded from the dead man's coat. Coughing, Frank spun in a blind frenzy and slammed through a swinging door. He rubbed the dust from his eyes with the heels of his palms. As he leaned against the door, the two creatures pounded against the other side. He blinked and found himself in a decrepit kitchen.

A few piles of trash lay heaped in corners. A dark, empty refrigerator yawned by an open window. The torn curtains wavered from an outside breeze. The bodies behind him pushed harder, their fleshy hands slapping the wood behind his head, jarring his teeth.

"Help!" he yelled.

Frank's walking shoes slid in the grime on the linoleum floor as his resistance to the onslaught began to fail. Scrambling to regain traction, he managed to recover several inches. A pasty hand shot through the opening and curled fingers clawed at his elbow.

"Heel, right now!" Dr. Bower's voice shot through Frank's terror.

The weight on the other side of the door dropped away, and Frank plunged to the floor at his pursuer's feet. Throwing his arms up to protect his head, he waited to feel their cold, dead fingers grasp his skin.

"E-hem."

Frank lifted an elbow and peeked under the crook. The zombies stood slumped, chins to chests. Dr. Bower raised an eyebrow and waved for Frank to get up. The postman crab-crawled a few steps back before venturing an attempt to stand.

"Two dollars?" the doctor asked.

"Huh?" Frank said, brushing the dust from his gray trousers. "Your pets tried to kill me, and all you can say is 'two dollars'?" He pressed his fingers to his temples.

"They're not my 'pets.' They're experiments, and human beings. I treat them like family." Crossing his arms over his chest, Dr. Bower raised his chin higher. "I believe you have a piece of my property in your possession?"

"If that's how you treat your family, I'd hate to see how you treat your friends," Frank mumbled.

"Excuse me?"

"I said that's some family you've got there."

Spinning in a tight circle, Frank searched the floor for the small, brown package. The sooner he finished the delivery, the sooner the nightmare would end.

The box was missing.

"The kitchen. I'll bet it's in there," Frank said, snapping his fingers.

The doctor took two steps to the door before the postman blocked his path.

"Oh-no you don't. You're not leaving me alone with these things again." Frank shook his head and gestured to the two zombies. "I'll find it myself."

Slamming his hands on the swinging door, he shoved the wooden panel so hard it smacked the wall. A dusty plaque that instructed readers to 'kiss the cook' fell from a loose nail and clattered to the floor. A small smile spread over Frank's face as the door creaked closed behind him.

The kitchen had darkened. The clouds that were stalking him all day were creeping closer. They'd eaten the sun and were threatening to drown the rest of his route. Spying the package under an overturned chair, he remembered the mailbag lying on the lawn. He scooped up the box and spun on his heel. A container of kitchen trash bags lay next to the door. He pocketed one as a crack of thunder rattled a stack of broken plates.

Upon returning to the foyer, he found it empty. He looked past the open front door as the first raindrops spattered the dry dirt path.

A scream sliced through the house as a flash of lighting brightened the yard, causing him to cringe. He looked out at the sack of mail. The pieces inside the ripped bag's folds were protected from the incoming deluge, but the wayward letters underneath could be ruined in a puddle. A thunderclap punctuated a high-pitched shriek.

He surveyed the room. A tarnished poker leaned against a cobweb-covered fireplace. Gripping the handle, he hurried to the hallway where the scream had originated. For good measure, he picked up a green glass ashtray and held it as if he were about to pitch the ninth inning.

A lightning bolt illuminated three figures: two standing, one cowering in a corner. From the sizes, Frank guessed Edgar and the undead woman to be the upright forms. That left Dr. Bower on the floor.

"Help!" the doctor cried, his voice lost in a thundering boom. "They're out of control!"

"Leave him alone!" Frank shouted over the storm. He poked Edgar with the end of the fire poker.

The monster ignored the tap. Frank pressed harder, piercing Edgar's coat. The zombie continued his advance on the doctor. Skewering the dead man's back with the metal rod, Frank continued to push until the sharp end emerged from Edgar's chest.

"What am I supposed to do now?" Frank asked.

The zombie turned at the sound of Frank's voice and ripped the poker from his hand. The handle smashed the door of a glass fronted curio cabinet, shards raining to the floor.

"Hit him in the head!" Dr. Bower cried out.

Looking once at the heavy ashtray, Frank lifted it and slammed it onto Edgar's forehead. The large body stumbled and shook its head as if trying to regain its balance. Frank took a step forward and smashed the heavy object into Edgar's pale face. Bones cracked; fluid poured from the zombie's nose and mouth. The dead man collapsed to the floor and lay still. Frank stared at the heap and shuddered.

Dr. Bower grunted. Frank turned to see the man waving his walking stick at the stumbling, undead woman's chest.

"Don't hurt her!" the doctor yelled. "See if you can restrain her."

"Why would I want to do that?" Frank hefted the ashtray. "These things are crazy."

"Please." The old man parried with his cane. "She's my daughter."

Frank looked from the rotting face of the decomposing young woman to the frightened face of Dr. Bower. Their noses were similar, and they had the same deep, dark circles under their eyes. Their weak chins mirrored each other. After taking the time to notice, Frank saw the likeness. But the family resemblance didn't change the fact that the stumbling cadaver was dead.

"I don't think that's your daughter anymore." Frank stood behind the rotting woman and raised the heavy ashtray.

"Stop!" The doctor shoved the flailing corpse into the opposite wall. "You'll kill her!"

"She's already dead!"

A flash of lightning flared in the window. Dr. Bower's pleading eyes flashed behind his crooked spectacles before he resumed deflecting his daughter's advances.

Lowering the ashtray, Frank scanned the room. A tired, golden rope sash hung next to a moth-eaten, velvet curtain. He ripped the cord from its nail and hurried back to where Dr. Bower struggled with his daughter. The mailman looped the rope and circled it around the thrashing creature. Once its arms were immobilized, the doctor lowered his cane and staggered around the wriggling body to tie the unraveling ends in a knot. The fraying fibers sliced into the zombie's decaying skin. Stepping over Edgar, he dragged his daughter to the winding staircase and tied the loose ends of the rope to the heavy wooden banister.

"There. That should do it." The old man smacked his hands together as if he were dusting breadcrumbs off after eating a piece of toast. He looked into the dead girl's milky eyes. "Now you behave." He turned to face Frank and said, "Thank you for your help." He readjusted his glasses before adding, "You may go now."

Frank dropped into a sheet-covered chair and began to cough as a swirl of dust surrounded him. The movement drew the old man's attention.

"Sir, you aren't safe here," Frank said.

"Please, call me Bill." Dr. Bower stretched a bleeding hand toward the postman.

"You're hurt. Shouldn't you call a doctor?" Frank grabbed the man's wrist and twisted it, trying to get a better look at the wound. The storm had been spent to a crippled drizzle, and the light through the open front door was enough to see teeth marks on the doctor's liver-spotted forearm.

"It's an old wound." Dr. Bower yanked back his arm and pressed his free hand over the bite. "Nothing to worry about." A drop of blood seeped though his fingers. "Just pulled off a scab, that's all. Now, if you'll please leave."

Shaking his head, Frank stood and wiped the dust from the back of his pants.

"Whatever you say, but I still need to collect that two dollars from you."

The doctor coughed through a chuckle. "The money's in my sweater pocket." Blood oozed through the creases in his hand. "You'll have to get it."

Frank edged over and reached out his hand as if he were being forced to pet an angry rattlesnake. When his fingers clutched the damp money, he jerked his hand out of the dark hole and stuffed the bills into his own pocket.

"Now, could you be so kind and deliver the mail and leave?" Dr. Bower's face had grown paler. He fell onto the covered chair, as rasping breaths escaped his cracked lips.

Frank recovered the box from beside the fireplace and positioned it on the injured man's lap. He stood transfixed as the doctor fumbled with the sealed seams. A flash of dentures and a rip of cardboard revealed a spew of white packing peanuts.

Dr. Bower raised his ashen face and peered at the postman. "Don't you have a paycheck to earn?"

Frank shook himself from his trance and backed toward the front door. The dead woman moaned by the stairs. Losing interest in the retreating mailman, the doctor sifted through the packaging.

A board squeaked under Frank's foot, and the old man shifted his gaze to the door.

"Please make sure the door locks behind you."

Frank peeked around the jamb as he pulled the door closed. He thought he saw the old man's head loll to a sloping shoulder just before it closed. He pressed the lever and the door locked as Dr. Bower had requested. With a listless shrug, he gathered the wayward letters and dropped them into the pilfered garbage bag. The envelopes were damp, but the canvas had protected them from the worst of the downpour. He refastened the wet mailbag after securing the thin plastic around the rip. Water droplets seeped through his shirt and chilled his skin.

A loud thud sounded on the glass behind him and Frank turned quickly to see a frail hand wipe away a long strip of dirt from a filthy pane of glass on the front door. The palm slapped it again, moving in a downward drag.

A moment later, Dr. Bower's wrinkled face smudged the filmy smear. Throwing a hesitant glance back in the general direction of the house, Frank cringed.

"If he has a problem with the delivery, he can take it up with the postmaster," Frank mumbled to himself. "I've had enough."

He waved politely in the doctor's direction one last time and grinned a tight smile as he pulled a small brown envelope from his pouch. Slipping the two crumpled bills inside it, he sealed the flap shut and checked the box marked 'Postage Paid.'

THE DOG, THE DEAD MAN, THE POSTMAN AND HIS LOVER

RICK MOORE

Nick eased down on the brake pedal, bringing the postal delivery van to a halt. He killed the engine and removed the keys, slipping them in the pocket of his gray shorts. A light blue-striped, short-sleeved shirt completed his postal worker's summer uniform. He liked the way its tightly cut sleeves made the muscles of his arms stand out. The shorts were kind of geeky, but a few of the women he delivered to had openly admired his muscular legs, so he guessed he must not look too bad in them.

The van had large side mirrors, and climbing down from his seat to the road, he couldn't resist looking in one to appraise his reflection. He'd studied it long, and often. Even as a kid, before girls started sending him notes and having their friends ask him out for them, Nick had known his face was something special.

A few of his drinking buddies thought they were God's gift to women, but when it came down to it, they were all talk and no action. Nick didn't really believe in God, but if he did, unlike those other guys, he thought he'd make a pretty good candidate for the title. Why else would he be hitting so much prime pussy? All right, maybe some of it wasn't all that prime, maybe some of it was quite a bit past its prime actually, but with girls his own age somehow sensing he was commitment shy, and usually giving him the brush off five minutes after realizing he only wanted to get into their pants, he had to take it where he could get it. Didn't he?

And Gina Jenkins wasn't past her prime. Most definitely not. Well, most definitely not much. Early forties tops, with an ass and tits a women half her age would envy. Who cared about that weird mole she had on her eyelid.

Nick took the keys from his pocket and locked the van, then remembered he'd forgotten something and unlocked it again. He leaned back inside, grabbing his clipboard and the letter off the passenger seat. The letter could have gone in the Jenkins' mail box, located at the end of the street, but when Gina called saying her husband was down at the welfare office trying to sort out an error to his disability check, Nick kept the piece of junk mail just in case her skuzzy old man came home early, knowing he'd need a cover story to avoid looking suspicious.

He took a good look around as he approached the gate to the walkway leading to the house. It was kind of a rundown neighborhood, lots of low income housing, lots of old cars leaking oil on the road, several up on blocks, but he heard nothing and saw no one. Which was kind of weird. Usually the booming bass of a hip hop track could be heard, or there were kids running in the street, or old men sitting out in front of their houses, drinking a forty of beer. Must have been something good on TV, he figured, and continued on to the house.

On the gate there was a sign: **Beware of the Dog**. The letters for the **w** and **t** had faded to the point where their outline was barely visible. Gina said her husband Earl had repainted the sign last year after they got Rollo, but that he'd run out of paint before finishing, and balked at the idea of buying an entire can just to paint in two letters.

What kind of an idiot paints the letters out of sequence, anyway?

Beware of the D, would have made a lot more sense than putting **Be are of he Dog.**

"Freaking dumb ass," Nick muttered, opening the gate. The hinges squealed. Hadn't Gina's husband ever heard of WD40? Still, Earl's laziness had its advantages. Nick waited to hear the resounding sound of Rollo's bark. Ever since Gina had forgotten to tie Rollo up in the backyard last winter, and the dog had bolted past her when she'd opened the front door and ripped a hole in Nick's pant leg, the deal was that whenever she called him she was to immediately take Rollo outside and make sure the mutt was chained to his cinder block at the rear of the house.

Today, there was no low-throated *woof* from the backyard. Could the pit bull be asleep? Gina had said she was going to take him outside and feed him after tying him up, so maybe that was it. He better not be loose inside. If Rollo was in the house, Nick was going to be pissed.

He walked on, passing yellowed tufts of weed-strewn grass to either side, the path beneath his feet a network of cracks sporting yet more weeds. The front door was located on the side of the house, the path running past it to a weather beaten gate that led to the backyard.

Even from here, Nick could see that the front door was slightly ajar. He didn't like this, not one bit. He stopped and looked up at the house. The stucco was chipped and dirty, the closed window blinds caked with grime. God, that Gina was a slob. What the hell was he doing, banging this old broad, when he could have had any number of cute little young honeys? All he had to do was work them a little bit, put in a little effort, instead of expecting them to fall at his feet like the old gals did. Nick cast a glance back towards his postal delivery van. What if all this was a set-up? One time after they did it, Gina showed him the Desert Eagle Earl kept in the bedside table's top drawer. What if Earl had found out about them and made her call him, holding the gun to her head the whole time?

Leave, he thought. *Just turn around and leave.*

But goddamn if Gina didn't have the tightest, wettest pussy he'd ever had the good fortune to stick his dick into. And maybe this was all some sort of game, maybe he'd go in there and find her naked on the bed, legs spread wide, not saying a word, just waiting for him to stick it in.

Nick pushed through his unease, walking on towards the front door. Some things in life were just worth taking a risk over.

He raised a hand and knocked, chips of peeling blue paint crumbling beneath his fingers.

"Postal service," he called. "Special delivery."

He pushed against the door, peered in through the gap at the darkened hallway.

"Hey, Gina," he called. "Ginaaaa. Gina?"

No Rollo charging out at him. No Earl walking out of the shadows, semi-automatic in hand. So far so good. Nick stepped inside, clicking the door shut behind him. He started down the hall, heading for the stairs.

A sound from the kitchen drew his attention.

Lap lap lap.

What the hell was that?

Lap lap lap.

He walked the rest of the way to the kitchen, pushed open the door, and stepped inside.

Gina had put on the nightie she knew he liked to see her in, the semi-translucent one with black lace trim. For a heartbeat his eyes remained on her ass. Then he took in everything at once, his mind trying to make sense of it all, and failing.

She was face down on the linoleum, dark thick blood pooling around her head. Rollo looked up at him and licked his bloody chops, then dipped his head and resumed what he'd been doing when Nick entered the room.

Lap lap lap.

At the counter, next to a sink clogged with dishes Gina would never get around to, stood a naked dead man. What told Nick the guy was dead, was the spray of shotgun pellets embedded in his shredded flesh. Whoever got him must have done it up close and personal. Nick could see jagged shards of shoulder bone poking out through strips of blackened tissue. It wasn't the damage to his back that told Nick the man was dead so much as his face. He'd taken a scattering of shot all down the left side; the bones in his cheek and jaw smashed to pieces, resulting in a glistening mash of tissue, tooth and bone.

"What the fuck's going on here?"

There was really no need to ask. The answer was self-evident. The dead man was making himself a sandwich.

"I like white bread," the dead man said, speaking out of the right side of his mouth, sounding like he'd suffered a stroke.

I wike whike bwead.

"You like white bread?" he asked. "White bread's good, huh?"

The dead man dipped a large, bloody carving knife with a serrated edge into a jar of mayonnaise— it was the same jar Gina had used when making Nick a turkey sandwich last week.

He worked the knife around in the jar, turning the mayo pink as some of the blood on the blade mixed in with it. He slathered a thick coating of the light pink mayo onto his bread.

"My wife used to insist on whole wheat," he said. "Better for my body, she'd say." He turned and looked at Nick and gave him a lopsided grin. "But I don't have to worry about that now. Do I?"

What was in the large yellow plastic bowl the dead man dipped his hand into squelched between his fingers. A handful of the stuff was dumped onto a slice of the mayo-topped bread. The filling for the sandwich wasn't meatloaf or ham or any other kind of cold cut. Nick saw an eyeball in there. Saw what looked like raw liver and kidneys and various other less identifiable lumps of flesh. The dead man reached into the bowl a second time. The heart dripped juices through his fingers as he moved it across the counter and put it down gently on top of the other organs and flesh strips.

Nick looked back at Gina's body. There was more blood leaking out, and it was spreading slowly from beneath her torso.

The dead man made appreciative grunting sounds, and when Nick's gaze lifted, he saw why. The dead man had taken a massive bite out of his sandwich, and chewed as best he could, then rammed more of it into his mouth. Some of the filling squirted out and landed on Nick's left sneaker. He saw it was an eyeball—

Gina's eyeball he figured — even though he could only see the back of her head.

Rollo looked up. The pitbull with bloody jowls trotted over, and sniffed the mayo coated eyeball.

"Five second rule," the dead man said.

Rollo evidently agreed. He gingerly picked up the eyeball with his teeth, squashed it between them, and gulped it down with a slurp of his tongue.

Rollo then raised his head and sniffed the air. The coppery scent of Gina's blood must have been so enticing that he hadn't cared when Nick first entered the room. All that changed now as the dog inhaled through his wet, brown nostrils, getting a whiff of Nick. Maybe it was hardwired into the pitbull's DNA to instinctively react aggressively to postman sweat. Maybe Nick's unfamiliar scent lingered in the house after he'd left before, causing Rollo to identify its presence as evidence of an intruder.

Whatever the answer, the message in Rollo's hard black eyes was easy to read. *You are my mortal enemy*, those eyes seemed to say. *And boy did you make a mistake stepping into this room, postman, because now your ass is mine.*

Just in case there was any doubt about his feelings towards Nick, the pitbull made them clear. He bared his teeth, growling low in his throat.

"What about him?" Nick cried, pointing at the naked dead man. "He killed your mistress. He's the one you should be growling at."

"No smell of fear on me," the dead man said casually as he ate. "Not like you."

Rollo barked, teeth dripping saliva.

"Screw this," Nick said. "I'm outta here."

He turned on his heels, reached for the door handle, grabbed it, pulled the door open, and stepped into the hallway. He tried to slam the door closed behind him, but something got caught in the jamb and squealed. By the time he looked down and saw what that something was, Rollo had scrambled through the opening.

Nick howled as the dog sank its teeth deep into the meat of his right calf. Nick tried to use his other leg to kick the dog and free himself.

Big mistake. He connected with the pitbull's body, eliciting a yelp and loosening Rollo's hold, but lost his balance in the process. Falling to the right, he hit the floor hard. The clipboard with the letter under the metal clip was still in his right hand. With all the insanity back in the kitchen, he'd forgotten it entirely. When he put out his right hand to cushion his fall, the clipboard connected for an instant, edge first, then collapsed beneath his weight, doing nothing to slow his impact with the floor. The side of Nick's head smacked the floor hard, knocking him out cold.

Excruciating pain wrenched him up out of the darkness. The first thing he saw was Rollo, sitting patiently on his haunches a few feet from where he lay. A stab of white hot agony drew his eyes to its source. The naked dead man sat cross-legged on the floor, Nick's calf resting on his knee. He was using the serrated edge of the carving knife to slice off strips of Nick's calf muscle.

"One for you," the dead man said, placing a raw red sliver of flesh in front of the pitbull. Rollo wolfed down the morsel as the dead man went back to work with the knife. "And one for me..."

Nick clenched his teeth, fighting the urge to cry out, knowing his only hope was to maintain the element of surprise. He needed a weapon. Earl's gun was upstairs in the drawer of the bedside table. If he could get away, just long enough to get to it, it would be game over for the dead man and Rollo too.

Rollo was just a dog. One with some seriously fucked up sense of loyalty, but just a dog nonetheless. And the dead man? He was a zombie. But not the type they showed in the movies, devoid of all sense of what they were, but Nick had no doubt that a bullet through the brain would put him down, just like in the same movies.

But for now, the only thing he could use to defend himself was the clipboard; it would have to do. He moved his hand slowly, stretching his fingers, reaching out until he had a firm hold of its edge.

Unleashing his rage with a low-throated yell, he sprang up and batted the side of the dead man's head. Then, holding the clipboard on both sides, Nick used it like a bat to deliver blow after blow, jarring the dead man's head from one side to the other; left to right, right to left.

"You ever play Pong, asshole?" Nick yelled, delivering another whack upside the zombie's head, knocking it as far as the vertebrae in his neck would permit. "Well, this is Pong of the Living Dead, you fucker!"

The knife in the dead man's hand fell to the floor. That was when Nick should have dropped the clipboard and picked it up. That was when he should have remembered he faced two foes, not one, the second no less dangerous than the first.

Rollo's teeth ripped through Nick's face like a knife ripping through paper. The pitbull's massively powerful jaws snapped shut, his head shaking from side to side, frenziedly worrying at the skin his teeth had punctured, gouging a hole in Nick's face as a chunk of cheek-flesh tore free.

Nick raised a hand to fend off his attacker, and managed to get it around the dog's neck. He pushed and felt too much resistance and screamed as Rollo's teeth snapped down on his nose. His flailing hand touched a wooden handle; somehow amidst the signals of pain being sent to his brain and the sensation of blood flowing down his face, his tactile senses jumped to the fore, identifying the knife for what it was. He grabbed it, then raised it and drove the pointed tip deep into Rollo's ear. The dog went suddenly limp against him, jaws falling slackly open, releasing Nick from the vice-like grip to his nose. Sitting up he pushed the dead dog away from him. It felt like snot was running from his nose and over his mouth, but when he wiped the back of his hand across it, the flare of pain made him quickly draw it away. Not snot but blood, the back of his hand testified, when he looked at it.

He saw the tip of his nose drop out of Rollo's mouth and thought he was going to vomit.

Not yet, he thought. *Not until this is over.*

The dead man was still trying to regain focus after all those whacks to his head. Nick intended to use the upper hand to his advantage. The loop of Rollo's leash—a length of rope for taking him out for walks—hung over the banister at the foot of the stairs; he retrieved it. He tied it around the dead man's arms, securing them to his torso.

He picked up the knife and pushed the dead man onto his back, resting the knee of his damaged leg on the dead man's chest. Using the knife's serrated edge, he began to saw through the zombie's neck.

"That won't work, you know," the dead man said.

When the head was separated from the body, he knew the zombie hadn't lied.

"Told you," the head said, his voice a raspy whisper. "What now, friend?"

"What now?" Nick asked, hysteria creeping into his voice when he saw his hands were drenched with gore from his wet work. "I'll show you what now."

Nick stood up, leaning against the wall for support. His shirt was soaked with blood, both the dead man's and his own. Now that some degree of clarity was returning to his thoughts, he realized he'd better go clean up, then get himself to the nearest hospital. He flexed his good leg and drew back his foot, then kicked the dead man's head as hard as he could. It bounced down the hall, rolling through an open doorway that led to the living room, vanishing from sight as the darkness swallowed it.

From the corner of his eye, he saw something move, and gave it his full attention. The dead man's headless body had just sat up. Blindly, the hands groped, patting the floor until one landed on the half-eaten sandwich. Nick backed away, limping.

When the hand holding the sandwich stuffed it into the open neck cavity, Nick knew if he didn't get away right now, he was going to lose it. Somehow his mind had coped thus far, but the sight of two slices of white bread protruding from the top of the dead man's neck cavity was just too absurd to take.

Nick turned and hobbled away, in desperate need of water to splash on his face, and the respite, no matter how temporary, of a room in which nothing abhorrent had occurred.

He arrived at the master bedroom and pushed open the door. Inside he found several scented candles, obviously lit by Gina before encountering the dead man in her kitchen. The wicks were low, sitting in pools of liquid wax, the sputtering flames casting jumping shadows on the walls.

Nick limped through into the bathroom. What he saw in the cabinet mirror brought tears to his eyes. His face. His precious face; the one thing he loved more than anything in the world, was ruined. He could see his gold fillings through the hole in his cheek. And his nose...

Maybe a plastic surgeon could fix me up.

"Yeah right," he said, replying out loud to his thoughts, his voice a low mutter. "On my salary?"

Outside in the street, he heard screams. He hobbled to the window, using the sink for support. He made a space in the blinds with his fingers and peered outside through the opening. His postal van was sitting right where he'd left it; what seemed like a lifetime ago. In a way it was a lifetime. Between then and now he'd crossed a line and there was no going back to who he'd been before. It wasn't so much the events as a whole, as those that affected him directly. He wasn't sure he could live as the disfigured freak Rollo's teeth and the dead man with his knife had turned him into.

Out on the street, he saw the source of all the commotion. An overweight Latino woman in a summer dress three sizes too small for her, was huffing and screaming and casting glances back over her shoulder, as she ran from a man dressed in a suit that had 'Sunday best' written all over it. A suit for church perhaps, though most likely a burial suit. The man's face and hands had not weath-ered the elements well, possibly due to a cut-rate coffin.

If ever there was an argument in favor of opting for cremation over burial, the man on the sidewalk personified it. His skin was beyond desiccated, so tattered it barely clung to him, with a skull and fingers that gleamed where the flesh had flaked away. A meat cleaver was buried in his collarbone, but the skeleton man in the suit seemed unaffected, walking on casually behind the woman, one hand in his pants pocket, the other swinging by his side.

Nick was transfixed by her enormous jouncing breasts, finding the sight deeply comforting after all the unpleasantness. He watched them bounce and jiggle until a noise in the bedroom drew his attention. He moved away from the window. The bedsprings creaked, and when he got there he saw it was Gina, intent on keeping their tryst, the interruption of being killed of little obstacle to her.

"Nick baby," she said. "Do me, would ya? For old time's sake, do me one last time."

With the blinds drawn all he could make out was her outline. He picked up the nearest candle, winced when the heated glass it was inside touched his fingertips, and put it back down. He grabbed one of Earl's dirty socks from the pile of clothes on the floor and used it to lift the candle, then waved it towards Gina's outline on the bed, illuminating her. She'd climbed under the sheets, leaving everything above the waist fully exposed.

So it had been her eyeball in the sandwich just like he'd thought. Her liver and kidneys and heart, too, judging by the dark hollow cavity where her flat stomach used to be. *'Cause I never dropped any rug rats*, he remembered her saying one time when he'd commented on what great shape she was in. *Same reason my tits haven't sagged and my pussy's still got some grip to it.*

"Christ, Gina," Nick said. "Do you even know what's hap-pened to you?"

"Disgust you do I?" she asked. "Then get out of here. You ain't so special yourself anymore. Go look in the mirror. Take a good long look. I watched the whole thing from the kitchen door. Rollo fucked you up good. Made a real mess of that pretty little face you're so fond of."

"Go to hell, bitch," he said, but the force he tried to put behind his words only came out in a trembling whisper.

"You little pussy," she said. "Go on and get. I don't need you no more. I got all I need right here."

She pushed back the sheets to show that the dead man's head was between her legs, eager to impress with a variety of techniques. His tongue darted and lapped. It swirled, first clockwise, then anti-clockwise.

Nick walked around to the side of the bed.

The dead man's eyes shifted in his head, settling on Nick. "I like eating pussy," he said. "Pussy's good. You like eating pussy?"

Nick slid open the drawer in the bedside table and reached inside for Earl's gun. He couldn't live in a world where the dead came back to life, at least not with his face looking the way it did. Maybe that made him vain and shallow and empty, just like his mother said, but so what? At a time like this there was no point lying to himself. He put the candle on the table beside the bed and went and sat in the chair Earl probably used to put on his socks and shoes.

Nick watched Gina buck and thrash and crush her thighs against the decapitated head.

He put the gun to his temple. Found the trigger. Sought the courage to do what needed to be done. A thought popped into his head. His empathy center, typically inactive most of the time, suddenly skyrocketed. He wondered what would become of all the little honeys out there, even the not so little ones, like the big breasted Latina he'd seen fleeing the skeleton man outside in the street. Specifically, he wondered how grateful they'd be if someone stepped up to protect them, someone who'd blow a big fat hole through the head of whatever dead asshole was trying to take a bite out of them.

Very grateful, was his guess. Even if that someone sported some slight disfigurements? He thought so. This was a new world, with new rules, after all. And in that world a battle-scarred hunk like him, a man who faced down death and survived, might just find himself the hottest ticket in town. And when night fell, and they were in hiding, wouldn't they all be yearning for the comforting embrace of their protector's arms around them? Hell yes they would! He could have himself a regular harem.

"I gotta split!" Nick yelled, jumping up. He put a bullet through the severed head's bald spot, splattering brains all over Gina's curly thatch of pussy hair. "Gotta get to a hospital and get stitched up."

The head was definitely dead. One to the brain, just like he'd thought. The movies at least got that much right.

"Nick, you selfish little shit," Gina spat. "Another ten seconds was all I needed. Couldn't you tell how close I was? Couldn't you for once consider my needs before your own?"

Nick stood blinking, not understanding what she meant. He waved and tried to give her a goodbye smile but decided not to when all his damaged nerve endings became one connection and let forth a singular cry of protest. "Sorry, Gina, I gotta run. Say hello to Earl for me."

He dashed around the bed and gave her a peck on the forehead, careful not to get too close to her mouth. She'd been good to him over the last eleven months, and he felt like he owed her some show of affection, it being the last time they'd likely ever see each other.

She smiled, a hand reaching for his fly. "You're awful happy for a guy with a hole in his face and half his nose gone."

He backed away just as her fingers brushed against his crotch.

"It's my lucky day, Gina. Long as I look at it the right way. It's my lucky day. If I play my cards right, I might be up to my elbows in pussy come nightfall!"

"You're an asshole!" she yelled, shaking her head.

Nick rushed out of the room, hobbling due to his bad leg. He pulled open the front door and barged right into Earl. The bearded man didn't look in the least disabled. He was huge. Somehow he took the gun out of Nick's hand, turned it around, and aimed it at him before Nick even had time to realize what had happened.

"Pal," the big man said. "Your face sure is one sorry mess."

"You must be Earl," Nick said.

"Yes I am," the big man said. "Now do you mind telling me just what the fuck you were doing in my house?"

Nick smiled weakly, his voice jumping to a high falsetto as he gestured to the clipboard on the floor in the hallway. "Special delivery?"

UNDEAD DELIVERY

ANTHONY GIANGREGORIO

Harold Mitchell reached over and turned off the alarm clock before it sounded. His internal body clock had woken him before the radio alarm as it usually did.

Beside him in the full size bed, his wife snored loudly. As he glanced over his shoulder at her, all he could see was a large lump twice as big as the one he made in the bed.

Sliding out of bed as quietly as possible, he reached down for his slippers and began to walk out of the bedroom, to the bathroom.

When he was halfway there, a floorboard shifted beneath his pressing weight and a soft *creeeaaaak* filled the room.

"Quiet down, Harold! God, you have no respect for others," Helen hissed between clenched teeth.

"Sorry, dear," he simply replied.

Other than snorting in an annoyed grunt, Helen went back to snoring, as if she hadn't spoken.

Harold padded the rest of the way out of the bedroom and into the hallway, relieved when he didn't step on any more loose floorboards.

His clothes were already laid out on a small table and he quickly got dressed, then went into the bathroom to do what everyone does every morning.

When he was finished, he went down to the first floor of their small one bedroom house and prepared to do his chores before going off to work.

First he had to make Helen's breakfast and lunch so she didn't have to stop watching her 'stories' during the day. He would prepare dinner when he returned home from work, so he at least didn't have to deal with that meal at the moment.

When he was finished with the meals, he did a quick load of laundry and made sure Helen's clothes were set out for her on a small bedside table upstairs.

When he was through with that, he checked his wristwatch to see it was ten minutes to six. He had risen at five in the morning, as he always did, and now that his chores were done, he grabbed his sandwich from the refrigerator—one he'd made the previous night—and headed off to work, using his beat-up and worn down Honda Civic. It was rusting from the outside in and he tried not to look at Helen's brand new Cadillac in the driveway as he climbed into his old car. The door squeaked and shifted when he opened it and he saw that the upper pin holding the door to the frame was about to snap off. He could buy a pin at the auto store on his way home, that is if there was enough time. Helen didn't like it if he worked late and she had to wait for her dinner.

He pulled out of the driveway, and with one last look at his home, aimed the broken grille of the Honda to the freeway.

As Harold drove, he hummed softly. He was a cheerful man, despite all he had to put up with. He never gave it much thought to how he'd ended up in an abusive relationship with a hulking sow of a wife, and even if he did, he probably wouldn't want to dwell on it.

Harold was a postman for the city, and though the job was demanding, he enjoyed being outside and meeting people on a daily basis.

Though meek at home, he was very outgoing in the world and everyone who met him liked him.

He was just a likable fellow.

Twenty minuets later, he pulled into the parking lot and climbed out if his car. As he walked away from the Honda, he remembered he'd forgotten to grab his lunch so he went back, opened the door, and reached in. He didn't lock the car, for there was nothing even the most desperate car thief would want, including the car as a whole.

With a bounce to his step, he headed off to the building to begin work.

It was as he was 'throwing mail,' which is what he did to get ready for his route, by organizing the packages and letters so he would have a bundle for each section, that his cell phone rang. Looking at the screen, he saw that the number was for his house—it was Helen.

"Hello, dear, I can't really talk now. I'm at work. You know they frown on cell phone calls unless it's an emergency."

"This is an emergency, Harold!" she screamed into the phone.

Harold's heart began to beat faster as different scenarios flooded his mind. Was she sick, a heart attack maybe? Were his or her parents sick? Oh God, did one of them die? Her tone, she sounded so upset, it must be terrible. He quickly asked her what was wrong, his mouth suddenly dry.

"I can't find the remote control for the television!" she yelled into the phone in reply.

Harold sighed heavily, a small crack in his normally pleasant veneer showing through. "Did you check under the couch cushions?"

"Yes, and it's not there."

"Harold," the office manager called from the other side of the room. "No personal calls unless it's an emergency. That's going on your personal record if you don't hang up right now. I just gave a speech about that two days ago."

"Yes, Mr. Swanson," Harold replied. Then into the phone he said, "Helen, I just got in trouble with my manager, I really have to go."

"But what about the damn remote!" she yelled.

He sighed again. "Did you check under the couch itself? Maybe it fell off the table and was kicked under there last night when you were getting ready to go to bed."

There was a brief pause, some scuffling, and then Helen said, "You're right, it is under there. I can see it, but I'll need to get a broom to reach it."

"Harold, get off the damn phone!" Mr. Swanson snapped, his tone heavy with impatience.

"Yes, dear, well I have to go, see you tonight," Harold said, and as he was closing the phone, he could hear Helen calling out, "No, wait, what about dinner toni…"

Harold tucked the phone into his pants and was about to get back to work when Mr. Swanson stepped up to him. "Can I see you in my office, Harold, we need to have a talk."

Harold rolled his eyes inwardly and did as he was asked, knowing he was about to get a verbal warning.

It was two hours later and Harold was out delivering his route.

His mood had soured since arriving that morning.

He now had a verbal warning on his permanent record and worse still, he was being audited today.

As Harold walked his route, delivering to the homes and apartments, he had another man following him with a clipboard. The man's job was to evaluate Harold's efficiency. What aggravated him the most was that every now and then the man would write something in his notebook, and would then smile wanly to Harold.

He hated that smile.

And of course, because he was being audited, the mail was suspiciously 'light' today. It was always like that during audits. Where normally, he would have twenty to thirty bins of flat mail and another ten to twenty packages, today he had less than half that amount. He always wondered where the mail was being hidden and he knew it was, because tomorrow, when the auditor was gone, he would end up with double the mail for the day.

Through some light chit-chat, Harold found out that the auditor had been a letter carrier himself for just under a week a year ago, and had then transferred into the managerial section of the post office.

Harold knew what that really meant.

The guy couldn't hack it as a letter carrier and so had gone into management. And like so many other jobs out there, the ones who can't do the job, manage the ones who can.

Harold walked along the sidewalk, and then after delivering to a small, one family home, he walked back to the street, down the sidewalk, then up the pathway leading to the front door of the next house.

He glanced over his shoulder to see the auditor was scribbling away again.

Though he knew it wasn't a good idea, he couldn't help himself and said, "Would you please tell me what I just did that made you write something down?"

"It's nothing," the man said curtly.

"Come on, don't give me that, just tell me already."

"After I submit my evaluation, your supervisor will talk with you; it's not for me to say out here."

Disgusted, Harold turned and walked over to the auditor, and before the man could stop him, he pulled the clipboard from his hands and took a step back.

"Hey, give that back!" the man yelled like a child on the playground who'd had his ball taken away by a bully.

Harold wasn't listening, he was scanning the last sentence the man had written.

"Didn't walk on the grass. Went the long way around," Harold said as he read. He looked up at the man. "Seriously?"

The auditor nodded. "Yes, that's correct. On that last house you walked up the pathway to the sidewalk then around and used the next walkway. All you had to do is cut across the grass and you would have saved 8.9 seconds."

"I don't like to cut across people's grass, I find it disrespectful," Harold rebutted.

"Well, Harold, maybe so, but we need you to be as efficient as possible and cutting across people's grass and driveways is one way. Every extra step you take is one more than is needed to do the job correctly."

Harold frowned. "I've been doing this job for over ten years and I do it well. Where in the hell do you get off…" He stopped, realizing he was going to blow up. "Look, I'm sorry, I shouldn't have said anything." He handed the auditor back the clipboard. "I'm sorry I took this."

The auditor merely frowned and began scribbling again as soon as he got his clipboard back. Harold rolled his eyes and resumed his route.

It was near the end of the day, an hour to go when the auditor stopped walking and called out to Harold. "Okay, I have every-thing I need. I'm leaving now."

"Good," Harold muttered under his breath, but he merely smiled at the man. As the auditor turned to leave, he stopped, and in his eyes there was a little bit of mischievousness. He knew he wasn't supposed to tell Harold any of his findings, but after what Harold did to him earlier, he couldn't help himself. 'Payback was a bitch' as the saying went.

"I just thought I'd let you know, Harold, that I believe you could easily have another ten streets added to your route if you simply did the job better. I'm recommending your route be ex-tended. As you know, the post office is cutting manpower and some routes need to be absorbed into others. If you take the north side of Route C into your own, that would mean the other carriers could take the others sides and…wallah…one less route to worry about."

Harold said nothing, knowing it would be fruitless, but deep inside he wanted to scream.

This man knew nothing. The mail was light today and to top it off it was a beautiful sunny day. Try doing the route in the rain, or in the snow, when half the pathways weren't shoveled and there was no place to park. Harold had more than fifteen hills on his route and each one was a nightmare to climb when it snowed.

"Well, anyway, take care, Harold, it was nice meeting you today, best of luck in the future," the auditor said and turned and walked away, whistling a tune as he went.

Harold stood still for more than five minutes as the auditor walked away and disappeared around a corner. He was so angry he wanted to explode. The saying, 'Going postal,' came to mind.

But Harold was a kind man, and as soon as the anger rose, it went back down, buried deep within his psyche.

With a weary sigh he turned around to get back to work, knowing when he got home that night, he had dinner and cleaning to do for Helen. If he didn't, she would yell and scream at him and basically make his life more miserable than normal.

As he spun around, he idly wondered how his life had become so difficult, but then any further thoughts were shattered from his mind when he saw what was now standing before him.

The only word to describe what was standing in front of him was a *zombie*.

Yes, that's right, an honest to God living dead person.

Harold could see where the zombie had walked out of the backyard of the house on his right, the shrubs were broken and damaged, leaves on the grass and walkways from where the zombie had pushed its way through.

It was tall, nearly a foot taller than Harold and had wide shoulders and thick muscles beneath its weathered and dirty shirt.

Its hair was sparse and seemed wet against its skull…or was that slime or pus?

Its head seemed oversized, or perhaps the skin had just shrunk against the skull, but none of that mattered at the moment.

The zombie was standing still, looking at Harold as if it was a cat and he was a mouse…a small mouse…a tasty mouse.

Slowly, the zombie leaned over and opened its mouth, a load roar ensuing. Harold had mail in his hands, and as the zombie roared, he found the mail was flying into the air as he freaked out.

A fucking zombie! he thought. And if it was like the ones in the movies, then it wanted only one thing…to fucking eat him!

Harold turned and ran, the mail flying out of his sack as he dashed down the street and into a front yard three house down. Breathing heavily, he looked back to see the zombie was still standing in the same spot…it wasn't following him.

He waited for a full minute, his heart pounding in his chest, and though he knew it was crazy, he began to walk back to the zombie.

When he was a few feet away, he stopped and looked at the animated corpse, one foot ready to slap concrete if he needed to escape.

The zombie didn't move.

"Uh, hi there, big fella. What's your name?" he asked like he was talking to a stray dog.

The zombie merely growled, saliva dripping from the corner of its mouth. Harold's nose wrinkled from the scent of rot and decay. The odor was sickly sweet and each time the wind shifted, he had to fight down the urge to retch. Still, bile crept up into the back of his throat.

"Uh, I'm Harold. Are you going to try and eat me, Mr. Zombie?"

No reply…obviously.

Harold scratched his head, wondering what was going to happen next. Though intimidating as hell, the zombie didn't seem to be threatening him. He looked around the street, not knowing what to do. He guessed he could go to the house the zombie came out of the yard from, and knock on the door. He could say, "Hi, did you lose a zombie? I found him wandering around." Hell, he might even get a reward, a tip.

Then the zombie raised its right hand and opened its mouth a little, the hand cupped so the fingers were pressed together. It moved the hand back and forth to its mouth. It only took Harold a second to figure out what the zombie was trying to tell him.

"You're hungry? Oh my, Uhm gees, if you eat what I think you're supposed to eat, I don't know what to tell you," he said with a frown.

His cell phone buzzed and he reached for it on instinct. "Hello?" he said absently.

"Harold? What are you doing for dinner tonight? I'm starving. The second you get in tonight I want you to make dinner. And I spilled coffee all over my favorite muumuu, I need you to do another load of laundry. Oh, and the toilet is filthy. I had one of my 'episodes' and it splattered under the seat. It needs to be cleaned. It must have been that four bowls of Raisin Bran I ate last night before bed. Harold, are you there? Do you hear what I'm saying to you? Harold?"

"Uh, yes dear," he said idly and hung up on her. He wasn't listening. An idea had popped into his mind like a freight train crashing through a brick wall.

It was evil, devious and downright mean, but the more he thought about it, the more it made sense.

At that exact moment in time, as Harold stood before the zombie, he decided it was time for a life change.

It was just after six when Harold entered his kitchen through the back door by way of the garage. As he stepped into his house and took of his jacket, he could hear the television on in the living room.

"Harold? Is that you?" Helen yelled through the house.

"Yes, dear, I'm home," he called back.

"Good, I'm starving, get to work making dinner!"

"I have a surprise for you, dear, do you want to see what it is?" he called.

"Yes, but bring it in here. I'm watching Oprah and I don't want to get up."

Harold grinned malevolently, the look seeming right at home on his once kind face.

"Not a problem, dear, I can do that."

He walked back to the garage and then returned to the kitchen a few seconds later. In his right hand was a rope and connected to the rope was the zombie he'd come across on his mail route. The zombie's hands were tied and there was duct tape on its mouth.

On the way home, the zombie had tried to take a bite out of Harold so he'd quickly taken precautions. It had been evident after being with the zombie for a while that it had been trained like a dog to eat only when told to, though like a hungry dog, if it went without food for too long, it might snap at a hand holding a sandwich.

Harold untied the zombie's hands and slowly peeled the duct tape off, not wanting to be rough, though he was pretty sure the zombie didn't care. Bits of flesh came off with the tape and there was a slight layer of pus and blood connected to the adhesive side.

Harold pointed to the living room, and then mocked that he was eating by placing his hand—with fingers pointed and closed—to his mouth and moving it back and forth to mime eating. The zombie looked at him and cocked its head, then seemed to understand what he was telling it.

Harold got behind the zombie and gave it a gentle push to the living room, while calling out, "Are you ready for your surprise, Helen?"

"For the last time, yes. Now where the hell is it? Bring it in here right now. I can't wait to see it," she replied.

"Oh, I have a feeling you're gonna love it," he said under his breath with a sly grin on his lips.

Harold watched the zombie cross the kitchen floor, stumble down the small hallway, and disappear as it turned into the living room.

At first there was no sound other than the television, but then an ear-piercing scream rent the air, followed by the sound of tearing meat, as if a butcher was separating the bones of a large rack of ribs by tearing each one apart with his bare hands.

As the screams began in full force, and Helen cried out for help, Harold went to the refrigerator and grabbed a beer. Then, after making sure the back door was wide open as well as the garage door, and after tossing some mud on the floor near the entryway, he called the police to report a zombie attack.

AUNT MAE'S FUNERAL

J. L. PETTY

"Dearly beloved, we are gathered here today to celebrate the memory of Mae Carter." The reverend adjusted his bifocals. She was a beautiful person, on the inside, as well as the outside."

I could feel the cold air on the nape of my neck. Aunt Mae's ivory casket slowly lowered into the ground. My eyes were blood shot red and sore. Memories of Aunt Mae played in my mind like newsreels… I couldn't ignore them. I kept seeing her face in my mind.

There was a young woman singing *Amazing Grace* by her tombstone. The woman had red hair and was wearing a black dress; with matching leather gloves. Her rendition of the song brought me to tears. *It was so beautiful.*

It started to rain. I could feel the fat splashes on my face. *Aunt Mae, I'll miss you and will always remember our good times together. God, take care of her.*

My thoughts were interrupted by thunder erupting in the clouds from afar. A lightning bolt slashed across the sky. The air felt moist and the trees danced back and forth in the wind.

"Mae was such a wonderful caregiver and…" The reverend paused. "Sweet Jesus, what in God's name is that?"

The tension in the air was so thick it could be sliced down the middle with a knife. The reverend's eyes were as big as saucers.

What's he looking at?

I scanned the entire graveyard. I saw nothing but family and the rest of the funeral party. The reverend removed his eyeglasses and pointed behind us. "There…over there." A few feet away from us, a miniature hand was reaching out of one of the grave plots. It was grabbing for something unknown.

"Someone help…I think someone's been buried alive." My cousin Jenny turned to walk to the grave but my uncle grabbed her hand. She stopped dead in her tracks. "What's the matter with you, Uncle Tim?"

"Look!" He pointed.

The head of a little girl popped out of the dirt, revealing stringy pigtails laced with blue ribbon. Her marble tombstone fell over and cracked right down the middle, splitting in two.

The girl's skin was ivory and pale. She had dark circles under her eyes, as if she hadn't slept in years. She slowly raised herself from the hole, revealing her decayed arms.

Her freakish appearance startled the entire funeral party. Everyone gasped and ran about the graveyard, like ants running from bug spray at a picnic.

My feet were glued to the ground and I couldn't close my mouth. The young girl charged at the reverend and myself like a bull in rage. Her yellow, polka-dotted, sunflower dress was torn and maggots fell from her mouth, nose and ears.

I couldn't move…

My knees were trembling. They knocked together. I was frozen like a statue in a wax museum. The reverend made a heroic leap in front of me, as if he were Superman. He was holding a leather bible and clutching a silver rosary.

What's he doing?

"Yea, though I walk through the valley of the shadow of death, I will fear no evil: for thou art with me," he said in a strong voice.

Ignoring him, the corpse tackled him like a football player in the Super bowl. The reverend fell backwards onto the wet grass and he cried out. He dropped his leather bible and his silver rosary on the wet grass as his arms went wide.

Upon falling, the preacher used his arms like a protective shield around his face.

With what seemed like superhuman strength, the animated corpse tore into him, as if he were nothing but a rag doll. She chewed on a limb, stuffing the warm flesh in her mouth, gnawing on it like a dog with a bone.

"Help me! The devil is with us!" The reverend squirmed on the ground like an earth worm. The girl sat on his chest and continued to eat his arm in front of him.

Panicked, I picked up a rusted shovel lying nearby on the wet grass. I swung at the young girl as if I were Babe Ruth. But my aim was off in my terror and the shovel merely glanced her head.

Damn it, I missed.

Irritated, she hissed at me; like an angry rattle snake.

The little girl had the reverend's blood staining her mouth like a clown in the circus, bits of meat stuck in her yellow teeth. The preacher laid on the wet grass, bleeding to death. He had an embrace of death in his eyes as he stopped struggling.

Suddenly, I felt ice cold hands on the back of my neck and the prickly hairs on my body stood up. I spun around quicker than a swirling toy top, my mind already guessing who it was behind me.

Aunt Mae, is that you?

I realized Aunt Mae's corpse had risen from her ivory coffin the same as the little girl. She looked like a store mannequin, her skin pale and lifeless. Her eye shadow was stained and runny, her red lip stick chipped and cracking on her dry lips. She smelled like a sack of old onions. Her silver wig was crooked and the pearls around her neck were tangled around one another.

What's happening? This is impossible!

I almost gagged when one of her blue eyes popped out of her head, black fluid oozing from the gaping socket. She moaned and drooled uncontrollably, reminding me of a newborn baby.

I dropped the rusted shovel as she came at me, taking hold of my jacket.

"Aunt Mae, stop! Don't do it!"

"Davey, come and die with me." She hissed as she continued clutching onto my clothes.

"Aunt Mae, please don't kill me. I'm your nephew, David. Don't you remember? I love you."

I was ignored.

I felt the hands of other zombies grab me from behind. I glanced over my shoulder to see a zombie in a postal uniform, his shirt black with dried blood, his thin hair hanging off his scalp, his mouth stained red with blood from a recent kill.

This can't be happening? It just can't!

Aunt Mae grasped tighter around my neck. "Come be a part of our family, Davey!" she whispered, her voice hoarse from the grave.

More corpses rose from the soil around me. The zombies grabbed at my leather shoes as Aunt Mae pulled my body backwards. Her dead eyes were void of emotion. Her mouth was wide as she prepared to take her first taste of my warm flesh.

I kicked at the zombies, but it was no use. Aunt Mae bound me tightly in her grasp and managed to drag me down into the grave with her, the others following.

I had thought I was attending my aunt's funeral today, little did I know it would be my own as well.

A NEW WORLD ORDER

SUZANNE ROBB

Mark Jensen hated his job. He stood at the front of the classroom, staring down at one of the most terrifying sights ever in his opinion.

Before him sat over a dozen children between the ages of eight and sixteen. He had been through this before, but it still didn't ease what he knew would be coming.

Since the end of the Zombie War, all the liberal, dirt-eating, tree-hugging hippies had wanted to find a way to use the zombies in some beneficial way to society. Two words described it: total lunacy.

People were quick to forget that zombies liked to eat brains, tear flesh off bone, and were overall disgusting creatures that were best left dead. Of course, no one would listen to Mark, he was just a PR guy after all, and before that he'd been a janitor, but had lost it to a so-called rehabilitated zombie.

The leader of the reintegration coalition had emphasized the importance of allowing zombies to be given the chance to become contributing members of society. He had to laugh at the idiocy of people having to smile at zombies delivering their newspaper or mail, or using the more feral of the bunch as security systems for the rich and famous.

Mark wanted to point out that the country was in a recession, and that jobs were at an all time low for those who actually had a pulse. How in the hell were people supposed to embrace the undead to do jobs that could be done by fully capable *living* Americans?

Mark went to the desk when the bell rang, and prepared to start his opening speech. This was the part he hated; pre-written propaganda-filled crap that he had to recite several times a day.

He spouted the benefits of zombies in society, as well as why there was no reason to be afraid. As someone who had gone toe to toe with them, he knew there was plenty of reason to be afraid. God, he hated liberals sometimes.

"Good morning, class, I'm Mr. Jensen and today I'll be talking to you about zombies." He waited as the room fell silent.

"As many of you know, and some of you might have already seen, zombies are being re-introduced into the population to help out with various jobs."

A hand went up.

"You in the back?"

"My dad said that zombies are dead, and should be put down. He doesn't want their decomposition ass near him." The boy was about seven, and obviously had a smart father.

"Well yes, zombies are technically dead, but they have a virus, so they really can't help it. If one of your friends had a cold, would it be fair to stop being friends with them because of that?"

Most of the heads shook no.

"In the future, more and more zombies will be among us. They will take on roles such as janitors, garbage men, DMV workers, hazardous waste clean-up crews, nuclear power plant workers, and road kill collection units. They will significantly improve our way of life by doing jobs that are dangerous, or simply below us." Another hand went up.

"Yes?"

"Do zombies poop? I mean they eat all sorts of crap, but I've never seen one poop."

There was one in every class.

"Contrary to what you might have seen in movies and the like, zombies do in fact have to expel what they eat," Mark explained. "They do not however 'poop' as we do. What happens is that since they're dead, their organs no longer work. When they have eaten enough to rupture their stomach, they'll start to expel food from a hole in their side, usually their belly button."

A group *'ewwww gross'* went around the class. He was in total agreement. It was disgusting, and to actually see it happen, or step in it was one of the most barf-worthy experiences a person could go through. He remembered the first time he stepped in zombie poop. It was full of undigested fingers, toes, and an eye. He even remembered the eye was blue.

"Yes, it is disgusting, but the re-integrated zombies have been fitted with special underwear that will collect their bodily fluids. This will help with keeping things nice and clean. Now, as I was saying, zombies 'will' be among us, and you need to know what to do, and what not to do." Mark took a deep breath for the next part. This was where he stopped brainwashing the poor kids, and blatantly lied to them. He gritted his teeth, and moved forward with his little propaganda machine speech.

"Now when the zombies first appeared they were sick, and didn't know what they were doing. What we found out was that with a little guidance and some behavior modification, they could be as harmless as kittens."

Another hand went up.

"Yes?"

"My mom said this whole thing is a bunch of hooey, and that the government is washing our brains." Mark got the point, and was happy to see another smart parent existed.

"There is no brainwashing here, I promise. All I'm going to do is give you some tips on how to co-exist with zombies in a safe manner. One of the things you must remember at all times is not to get too close to one. Try to stay at least ten feet away from them at all times, and no matter what, don't accept candy or anything else they might be trying to offer you."

Mark looked around the room to make sure they were all paying attention.

"Another important thing to remember is that if one grabs or bites you, tell someone immediately."

A hand went up.

"Yes?"

"I thought you said they were harmless? Why would one bite us?" a boy asked.

"Well, it's kind of like a dog," Mark replied. "Most dogs are good, but on occasion you get a bad one that bites or attacks someone. The same concept applies to zombies, while most of them have been thoroughly checked out and deemed safe, it is possible that one might slip through. Don't worry though, it's very unlikely, especially if you remember to keep your distance." Mark looked down at his papers, and took a steadying breath. "Lastly, if you suspect that someone you know has been bitten, you must report it as soon as possible. We wouldn't want another outbreak to occur, right?"

The entire class nodded in unison. With his speech finally done, he now had to do the awkward part. He found that kids asked the more important questions that politicians seemed to skim over.

"Okay, now I'll take a few questions from you." All hands went up; Mark was expecting that.

"Okay, let's start with you in the front." He pointed to a little girl.

"My grandma is a zombie. Can I still play tea party with her?" she asked in a sweet voice.

"That might be a bad idea. But it's up to the discretion of your parents."

She was a goner.

"My brother said that zombies eat you if you make Santa's naughty list," a boy asked.

"Well, you can tell your brother that he's wrong, we all know that it's the elves that eat you," Mark laughed and two kids started to cry. "I'm just kidding, there's no Santa, you're brother is just being silly."

Three more kids started to cry.

"What I mean is, there is a Santa, but he doesn't do anything about the naughty list. Okay, next question."

A twelve-year-old boy spoke up. "My dad told me it's the damn hippies fault that we have to live with zombies now, and that if zombies tended their pot farms they would change their mind." This kid was speaking to his soul.

"Well, yes the liberals did play a big part in making sure that zombies were given equal rights, and job opportunities, but we all voted on it in the end," Mark said.

It was a close vote, too. Mark was sure it had been fixed due to the fact that zombies were allowed to vote. There were approximately 10,000,000 zombies in America. That significantly swayed the numbers in favor of the un-dead agenda.

"Can zombies have babies?" a girl of nine asked.

"No, as I said earlier, zombies are technically dead therefore they cannot in fact have babies." Mark didn't mention that he'd seen Zombies trying to 'make' babies, and as a result his testicles almost fell off.

"Do zombies like puppies?" a little girl with pigtails asked.

"Zombies like all animals, but it's better not to let them play together," he answered.

"Why?" another student asked.

"Because it isn't a good idea."

"Why?"

"Because I said so."

"Why?"

"Because zombies can get too playful and hurt a puppy, or a puppy can get too frisky and nip a zombie."

"My daddy says this is going to screw the social security system right into hell."

Okay this was a tough one to answer. This was an adult question and Mark wondered if the kid was a plant of some kind. The right answer was that, yes, social security was screwed, people that had died, and stopped receiving benefits were now eligible to get them again; family members were coming out of the woodwork to help their new zombie family members manage their money.

The other problem was that zombies were getting paid minimum wage for whatever job they were doing and they paid almost nothing back into the social security program. Since they lived forever, it didn't take a genius to figure out that social security was screwed.

"I don't know about that," Mark said. "I think it's premature to jump to a conclusion like that until all the facts are in." He gave the stock reply that was scripted for a situation like this.

"Do you like zombies, Mr. Jensen?" another student asked.

Time to go.

"Well, sorry, kids that's all the time I have today for questions. I hope you learned something, and most importantly remember what I said. Stay away from them, and don't accept candy or other small items they may try and give you. Have a great day."

Mark grabbed his notes and left the room as quickly as possible. He went straight to the parking lot and got into his car. As soon as he entered his car, he took out a bottle of sedatives. He tossed four in his mouth, swallowing them dry.

He'd been taking the pills ever since the whole zombie thing started. There was a significant rise in PTSD, anxiety, panic attacks, and agoraphobia over the last year. He'd only been experiencing anxiety attacks so far, but he knew as soon as he started seeing those rotting carcasses mowing his lawn, or delivering his paper or mail, he was going to lose it.

He believed in fairness and equal rights. Hell, he even thought women were entitled to equal pay. He'd considered himself a left wing nut before this all happened but now he was running with the Republican crowd, and saw the dangers the liberals presented.

That kid in there was totally right when he said hippies would hum a different tune if zombies were harvesting their pot plants. Mark was pretty sure if that ever happened, there would be a march on Capitol Hill to rid Mother Earth of the rotting menace led by a guy with flowers in his hair, wearing a skirt, and waving a hemp purse.

Unfortunately, until something went horribly wrong, like people being eaten and massacred at large, there was nothing to be done. So he sat in his car, ate his sedatives, and tried to visualize his happy place. This was hard to do because his cabin was his happy place, and that's where the zombies first appeared.

He decided he wasn't going to any more schools today. He'd led enough children down the path of death for one day. He hated doing it, but a job was a job after all. Soon enough, people who were alive were going to lose their jobs if they didn't give up their dental, optical, and any other health benefits they had. Zombies didn't ask for those, so they saved companies millions of dollars.

Mark assumed insurance companies would have lost their revenue over this, as milking the working man of his money was their bread and butter. However, now they had a whole new system to milk. The zombie insurance program was in its beginning stages, but would soon become a money maker.

Essentially, how it worked was the worker paid an obscene amount of money for a policy that stated if you were killed by a zombie, turned into a zombie, or attacked in any way by a zombie, they got paid a whole lot of money, or their family did.

What people didn't read in the small print, was there had to be four witnesses to say the deceased didn't start the fight or attack, and that if they had any sort of anger issues or a past criminal record, the policy was instantly voided.

Zombies also made the ideal employees because they didn't complain about working on holidays, working overtime, and didn't even think to ask for a raise. They were just about the perfect employee. Mark hated zombies, they made real people look bad.

As he sat in his car, waiting for the sedatives to do their magic, he thought about the public as a whole. He was not the most educated man. There was just no way he could understand how the public as a whole was swallowing the load of *re-integrated zombie* crap.

He wondered just how aware the general public was when it came to the jobs zombies got hired for. There were the ones that he talked about. The ones that put a kind face on the walking dead.

There were the jobs where they delivered papers, the mail, mopped floors, handled hazardous materials, unloaded toxic waste and the like. But did the public know about the dirty under-belly of zombie jobs?

Did the public know that medical schools eagerly accepted the un-trainable zombies for their anatomy courses? Performing autopsies on them over and over again. How about the use of zombies for colonizing bacteria and other nasty viruses for use in germ warfare should a world war ever break out.

He knew that the public didn't know about those jobs. Then of course, there were the jobs given to zombies by people who pur-chased them on the dead market. Funeral homes were a large player in that game.

Want Aunt Betty cremated? No problem, we'll do it for you. The only problem was they used zombies to take care of the bodies, and handed back an urn full of fireplace ash. It was cost efficient, but Mark was pretty sure families wouldn't be okay with that particular truth.

The worst use for zombies he'd heard of so far was bill collect-ing. Apparently credit card companies had tired of hearing the same excuses from people as to why they couldn't pay their bills. As a way to combat this, bill collectors now left zombies in a person's car, truck, or home until they paid their debt.

To Mark this was the worst job, because there was a zombie living in his house right now, forcing him to live in his car. He had no intention of paying off the loan at the moment either, because he knew his house was now full of zombie germs…and zombie poop. Right about then the sedatives kicked in and he went to sleep.

Saturday night found Mark eating at his favorite diner. He or-dered the special: meatloaf with a secret sauce. While he ate, a shadow passed through the front door. He looked up to see his old friend Steve walk into the restaurant, and stop in front of his table. Mark waited a moment, then Steve came over and sat in the seat across from him. He pulled a gun and put it to Mark's head.

"Hey, Steve, I'm still alive, you can put the gun away."

"You sure? You been bit, attacked, come into contact with anything?"

"I'm sure on all counts."

"Okay, good, just had to be sure. So how are things?"

"Fantastic, I'm living in my car because I lost my job and couldn't pay my mortgage. Now a zombie is crapping in my living room. I had to take a new job as a PR mouthpiece, promoting the acceptance of zombies in society. And right now my best friend just held a gun to my face, so things really couldn't be better."

"Huh, that sucks. I got a zombie living in my car. I got fired from the scrap yard and was replaced by one of those things. Then my wife left me. She claims I have issues or something. I could use some help if you know what I mean."

"Look, you can order something to eat, but that's it. I'm strapped for cash, too. Did I mention I can't pay my mortgage?"

"Hey, you owe me, man," Steve said.

"What are you talking about, I don't owe you anything."

"I didn't kill you did I?"

The waitress came over to the table, her body armor quite visible beneath her uniform. She looked at the two men and raised an eyebrow. "Are you gonna order something? You can't just sit here if you don't eat," she said to Steve.

Steve picked up a menu and looked it over. "Cheeseburger, well done, fries on the side with mayo." The waitress wrote down the order, then took away the menu.

"There, I just got you a cheeseburger for not shooting me," Mark said.

"Come on I was just joking. But you do owe me."

"See, you just lost me again. Do you want dessert or something?"

"No, you moron, I want you to join my team."

"How does me owing you have anything to do with me joining your team? And what team are you talking about? Bowling, softball? Sorry but not interested," Mark said.

"Fine then you have to make this up to me."

"What? Are you my girlfriend all of a sudden? I forgot an anniversary and you won't stop harping about it until I pull a diamond out of my ass?"

"Something like that," Steve replied. "I'm with a group of people. They know the truth about the zombies. The truth about how the virus got out, and what they're really doing with them."

"That's great, but I don't owe you shit. In fact, if I recall you owe *me* money."

"Work with us and we can expose this whole 'zombie in society' thing as a sham."

"It's not a sham," Mark said. "Zombies are members of society, and soon they'll be all over the place."

"Come on, you know they can't be trusted."

"No kidding, of course I know that."

"So help us," Steve said.

"Exactly how am I going to help you? I make speeches to little kids. It's not like

I'm lunching with the ACLULD."

"Don't even talk about them with me. If it wasn't for those hemp-smoking-flower-loving-hippies, we wouldn't be in this mess. The American Civil Liberties Union for the Living Dead would never have gotten involved."

"That's one thing I still don't get," Mark said. "I mean, the zombies ate thousands of people, infected thousands of people, still present a danger, yet the liberals are protecting them. It makes no sense."

"Exactly, that's what me and my associates are talking about. We know the truth. Join us and help."

Mark felt like the star of a bad movie, but became intrigued nonetheless the more his friend rambled.

"Explain how I can help," Mark said.

"You have access to the main LDR building. If you can help sneak us into the Living Dead Relations building, we can tap into their system, and find out what they're really up to," Steve explained.

Mark was pretty sure, positive in fact, that joining up with Steve and his friends would be a mistake, but he had nothing else to do and nothing left to lose.

"I thought you knew what they were up to?" Mark said.

"Well, we have an idea. We want to go in there and make sure we're right"

"All right, what the hell, I'll help."

"Great, we'll be in touch. Tell no one."

Mark was about to answer that he had no one to tell when Steve ducked under the table and started to crawl out of the restaurant. Apparently, he was trying not to attract attention. Ironically it worked, since the Zombie Epidemic, most people now had random quirks, tics, and tactics to avoid human contact.

A week later, Mark was sleeping in the back seat of his car. Images of zombies eating him flashed across his closed eyes. He woke suddenly when an incessant pounding scared the hell out of him.

Opening his eyes, he saw Steve standing outside his car. Mark sighed, opening the door. As he stepped outside into the parking lot, he stretched. He tried to buy time, knowing he wasn't going to like what Steve had to say.

"Okay, check this out," Steve said. "We got a plan and a crew together. All we need is for you to get us into the building and we're gonna blow this conspiracy wide open."

Mark looked at Steve, and noticed he had crazy eyes. He had to tread carefully here. He wasn't sure how off the rails his friend had gone.

"What conspiracy are you talking about?"

Steve gave him a hard look. "It's not for you to know yet. You're either in, or we break your legs."

"Well, when you put it that way, I guess I'm in."

"Fantastic, buddy, I knew we could count on you. Now gather all the supplies you need, and tonight we go in. Meet us in front of the LDR building at midnight. I'll send out a bird call to let you know where we are."

Mark nodded his head and watched as his friend dropped down, rolled underneath the car beside him, then pop up on the other side and break into a sprint to catch the bus.

What the hell had he just gotten himself into? Mark wondered.

Figuring he wouldn't be a free man tomorrow, he decided to live it up today. He took some of his sedatives, and had a few beers at one of his favorite local bars. He watched the hours tick by, getting sleepier with each move of the hour hand.

At eleven he switched to drinking coffee, figuring at least one person should have half their wits about them tonight, though he wasn't sure it would make much of a difference.

They were all going to get arrested, but at least he would get a room and bed.

The alarm on Mark's watch beeped, letting him know midnight had come and gone. He was standing outside the LDR building, trying to look casual. After waiting for five minutes, he heard what sounded like a duck call, or perhaps a duck being strangled.

"Psst, Mark, over here."

Mark raised an eyebrow and looked at Steve and two other men who were hiding behind a tree.

"Hey, guys, come on over here. Let's get this started shall we," he said.

"Mark, you have to be more careful; where's your gear? What are you wearing?"

Mark looked at Steve and his two friends. They were in full camouflage gear, had backpacks, and carried large duffel bags.

Glancing down at his jeans and white V-neck, Mark felt oddly overdressed to be busting open a conspiracy plot.

"Sorry about that, it's been a while since I broke into government property to crack a secret government plan."

"It's okay, buddy, I get it. Here, put this on, it should help a bit." Steve tossed a black sweatshirt which Mark barely caught.

He put the sweatshirt on and felt dumber than before. This was such a bad idea, but it was like a train wreck; he could not turn away. Watching as Steve and his buddies time synchronized their watches, he just shook his head.

Idiots, he was going to either die, or spend a good amount of time behind bars with utter morons.

"You ready, Mark? Get us into the building; go work your magic."

Mark motioned for them to follow behind him and they arrived at the front doors of the LDR building ten minutes later. They would have gotten there sooner, but Tim—one of Steve's friends—made them stop every minute to make sure they weren't being followed.

Mark looked at the lit path they were following and thought about how there were in a wide open place. The other guy didn't have a name; apparently he wanted to pretend not to have any associations with them if caught. His solution to that was not to tell them his name.

When they arrived at the front door, Mark swiped his key card. He had general access, which meant to the lobby and the main conference room for lectures every other Friday. The doors opened with a hiss and Steve, Tim, and No Name watched in awe.

"Dude, you have more power than I thought. Just how high up are you," Steve asked.

"Oh, I'm one of the highest." Mark laughed to himself at his own little joke, the sedatives not quite dulled by four cups of coffee.

The four men entered the lobby and Mark motioned for Steve to lead the way. Steve looked around, made a fist, then waved it in the air. The other two men instantly got down on one knee and pulled out a map.

"Okay, this is our location." Steve pointed to an **X** on the map. "This is where we're heading. We need to go that way." He pointed to a door on the west side of the room.

Mark had never been through that door before. Then again, he had no need to. It led to the back of the building where they kept all the heating and cooling equipment. At least that was what they told him.

"Okay, Mark, let's do this. Get that door open and we're halfway there," Steve said.

Mark smiled and walked over to the security guard sitting behind the lobby desk.

The LDR building always had a guard on duty in case of vandalism. Tonight it was George Harris; he was a bit older and tended to nod off.

This was one of those times, so Mark indicated to his friends to be quiet, then started to walk towards the door Steve thought was going to lead him to the land of epiphany.

When Mark reached the door, he swiped his card, thinking it would work fine. It was just boilers and air conditioners after all. When he saw the red light, he was caught off guard. He swiped it again, and once more received the red light.

"Mark, they're onto us. It was only a matter of time, we gotta move," Steve whispered.

Mark watched in horrific fascination as Tim and No Name pulled out a brick of C-4. They taped it to the door, stuck a detonator in it, then a wire which they let out for about twenty feet. Steve was holding the detonator when Mark said, "Steve, why don't we just blow the card reader, much less noise. Otherwise we'll have the guard on our ass."

Steve looked at him with an odd expression. "Where did you get so smart? Have you had military training?"

"No, I just don't want to die."

Mark exhaled as he watched Steve motion to Tim and No Name in some sort of weird sign language they'd developed. A much smaller amount of explosives used, meant a much smaller explosion.

When the small *bang* happened, George stirred in his seat, but didn't fully wake. The sound was no louder than a firecracker and George was a heavy sleeper. Mark again exhaled in relief. He knew if he was a cat he would only have about three lives left; he'd used most of them up in the Zombie War.

The four men, led by Mark, went to the door and opened it. When they entered the room, they all stood completely still. Mark had no idea what to do. It was as if he was living one of his nightmares.

They were in a warehouse, which in and of itself, wasn't a bad thing. What made Mark wet himself a little, were the dozens of zombies shambling around. They were filling boxes with fliers, loading boxes onto trucks, some were mopping, and others were doing nothing at all.

"What the hell is this, Steve?" Mark asked.

"This is what we're blowing sky high, buddy. Sorry I had to lie to you, but I knew you wouldn't go along with what we really had planned."

Mark stared at his ex-friend and wondered if he could kill him before the other two got to him. "What is your real plan then, *buddy*?" Mark asked.

"Well, this is the rehabilitation facility, this warehouse is where they keep the feral zombies that they're getting ready to train. My friends and I are gonna blow the place up, and send a message that we don't want rehabilitated zombies among us."

Mark was backing up, ready to go out the door and never come back, when he was stopped by something small in the center of his back. He turned to see No Name, and when he looked down, Mark saw a gun in his hand.

"Mark, you know too much, you have to see this through. It'll be fine," Steve said.

Mark had heard that before, many times, and every time it was never fine. He walked ahead, the gun in his back a good motivation, and they made their way through the creepy working dead.

Mark thought it was weird how not a single zombie noticed them, or looked at them, or acknowledged them. If it wasn't so ironic, he would have called them zombies if they were just normal warehouse workers.

When they arrived at the back door, Mark wanted to point out that it had a huge warning sign on it proclaiming ***ENTER AT YOUR OWN RISK***, plastered across it. Tim used a bit of the C-4 and got the door open. What they found on the other side, none of them expected.

They opened the door, and were greeted with the stench of death. It hung in the air and all four men gagged. They each reached into their duffel bags for a mask. Steve handed an extra one to Mark, who nodded gratefully.

The darkness was pierced by a flashlight held by Tim, and they all jumped back when they saw what was approximately five feet in front of them.

At least a dozen zombies were chained around the neck. They were skeletal, and Mark knew that meant they were security. The more starved a zombie got, the more feral it became. These were some of the fiercest.

Each of the men took out axes, swords, and a hatchet. Steve reached into his bag and handed a pocket knife to Mark, who looked down at it, raising an eyebrow.

Tim handed him the flashlight, and he held it on the zombies as the others went to work. No Name preferred to use his samurai sword to make quick efficient cuts. Of course the zombies looked like cold cuts when he finished, but whatever it took to get the job done.

Steve on the other hand liked to get up close, make a face at them, then use the hatchet to break them down bit by bit.

Tim wielded an axe like an expert. He beheaded, or in one case removed, all the limbs, and left the head. Mark didn't ask why, he could tell there were some underlying childhood issues that needed to be addressed.

"Okay, so that's taken care of. Now we should go into the holding room," Steve said.

"Should do, or will go? Just how well did you research this, Steve?" Mark asked.

"Relax, buddy, I did my homework."

Mark gripped the pocket knife tightly and relinquished the flashlight back to Tim. He walked behind the others, wanting to turn around and run, but he couldn't see and would most likely trip in the gore of the massacre.

The flashlight lit up yet another door. The warning was a simple one this time: ***ENTER AND DIE***. The three men in front of him opened the door, which wasn't locked. Mark wasn't surprised by this. Twelve of the fiercest zombies would deter most people.

As they entered the room, Mark realized Steve was right. The room held dozens of holding cages. Bony, fleshy arms reached out for them, and the smell made them all wretch. When they had control of their stomachs, Steve and his two friends got to work.

Bricks upon bricks of C-4 were pulled out of their duffel bags. They must have had at least a hundred pounds between the three of them. They placed the charges at the corners, in front of the cells, and wherever else they felt like it.

Mark watched in amazement at how well they worked; at least Tim and No Name. Steve just seemed to copy them.

That was when Mark realized they had used Steve to get to him. They needed one swipe of the card to delay the authorities. Mark could just imagine Steve bitching about his friend that worked in the LDR building, and these two zeroing in on him.

Mark thought about saying something, but then the fact that the lights were on and the fact that everything had been so easy flipped a switch for him.

"Hey, Steve, do you wonder why this has been so easy? Has it crossed your mind it's all a little too simple?"

"We had to kill those zombies, that wasn't easy."

"Steve, think about it, this has been way too easy. Something isn't right here."

At that moment, brighter lights went on, flooding the area, and applauding could be heard. Mark looked up to see the man who gave the lectures on Fridays. Marcus Winston, he hated him.

"Welcome, gentlemen, we've been expecting you," Marcus Winston said jovially.

Mark had a bad feeling start to bubble up in his stomach. Why were they expecting them? That was when he saw Steve walk over to the wall, and hop onto the ladder that led to the third floor where Marcus was.

"You? Seriously, you're the traitor? How does that happen?" Mark asked.

"Money, my friend, that is how this happens. Lots and lots of money."

Tim and No Name were talking amongst themselves, obviously not happy with the turn of events. Mark was trying to figure out why this was happening.

Then it dawned on him. Steve might say he was in it for the money, but that was too easy.

"What's the real reason, Steve? What's the going rate to sell us out to these guys? What are we going to be: food for the trainees? Perhaps we're going to become hapless victims in some weird accident?" Mark said.

Steve smiled. "Nothing that blasé, Mark, the liberals know there's hatred directed at them, and they need some sympathy press. Plus, they offered me a spot in the cabinet next election. Imagine the power. Imagine how good we're gonna look tonight, being able to say we fought off an organized military attack meant to start another Zombie War. The opposing party won't stand a chance. People will see us as the future."

"This has all been a set-up from the very beginning? For what, an election? You have to be kidding. You're playing with people's lives here," Mark said.

"Actually, I'm just playing with three lives," Steve replied.

A buzzer sounded and the doors on the bottom level cages opened. Mark looked down at his pocketknife and knew he wouldn't last long. He ran and hid behind Tim and No Name.

As the first wave of undead came at them, the two men in front of Mark fought bravely. Unfortunately, there were just too many foes. When the two men fell, Mark knew he was going down soon after.

He closed his eyes as they came at him.

He felt cold papery hands pull at him. He felt teeth bite into him and tear chunks of his skin away. Then an artery was torn, and as he hit the cold cement floor, he felt a warm pool of blood form around him.

He never screamed. He didn't want Steve to have the pleasure.

Jenny Richards hated her job. She used to be a receptionist, but was replaced by one of those damn zombies from the steno pool. Now she was a mouthpiece for the ACLULD.

She stood in the classroom and looked over the new papers she'd received. New developments in the rehabilitation movement meant that zombies were able to do more jobs now, making lives better.

Taxes were lower, because social security was gone. People were actually opting to become zombies when they died, so they could still contribute to society. The real truth was that people now had to work even after they died, in order to support their families and pay for funeral costs. It was all propaganda.

She heard she was replacing some guy who flipped out and tried to start another Zombie War a few months back.

She wondered how long until that happened to her. Her boyfriend Steve told her not to worry about it, but she couldn't help it.

HOW DO YOU EAT A WHOLE HUMAN?

DANE T. HATCHELL

"Really, Natalie, I think it'd be best if you brought the casserole over to the Canfield's," Bo said, scratching his five o' clock shadow. "You made it and everything. Mrs. Canfield's going to want to know the recipe and I don't want to get caught up in a thirty minute question and answer session about what you used to season the meat or how you sliced the carrots."

"But, Bo, I simply don't have time right now. I'm boiling the pasta, and I've got an organic pound cake in the oven that I've got to keep a close eye on. You know I can't trust you to watch things," Natalie said. "What's the big deal? You like Mr. Canfield. You used to hang out with him all the time before he became bed ridden. I bet he'd be thrilled if you just stopped in for a minute to see how he was doing."

"Yes, well, it's not like we were the best of pals or anything. We drank a few beers together in the afternoon sometimes. He liked to talk about his career in the Navy and I liked to hear his stories. We both like hockey and professional football. He's a nice enough old man, but he wouldn't let you get too close to him. He seemed distant, like he was passing time, waiting for death. I guess when you get that old, it's the next big event in your life."

Bo was tempted to tell Natalie the real reason why he didn't want to go next door, but didn't want to get into it with her right then.

"Go over and see him. It'll probably make his day. Just think, one day that could be you lying in bed with no hopes of ever living a normal life again."

Bo curled his upper lip. "If the roles were reversed, then I'd want him to bring me a gun. I'd get it over with in a hurry. I don't want to linger on for weeks or months, dragging everyone else down with me."

"Now you listen to me, Bo. Miles and Aubrey will be here in about an hour. So go on over there, get it over with, and get back in time to have a cocktail. I'll make you a double martini with blue cheese stuffed olives," Natalie said with a smile.

"Sold! I'll be back as quick as I can," Bo said eagerly while straightening his collar and checking his fly to make sure it was zipped. He grabbed the covered Pyrex dish and walked out the door.

He realized his mouth felt even drier now that he anticipated the icy coldness of crisp vodka passing over his tongue. He took the direct route down his driveway, across the sidewalk, and up the Canfield's driveway towards their front door.

He learned over two years ago not to make the mistake of crossing over the yard and going to their back door. The last time he did, he found Mrs. Canfield sprawled out in the nude on a lounge chair when he rounded the hedges.

Her stomach was so large and flabby that it hung low enough to cover her crotch. Her bosoms sagged down under her armpits like water balloons with blue veins winding over them like streets on a roadmap.

Bo had been daydreaming on his way over that day, and was more startled than she was when he came upon her. He remembered saying something like, "Whoa…Mrs. Canfield…I'm so sorry," and froze in his tracks, embarrassed, not knowing what move to make next.

A bigger surprise came when she smiled, revealing that she was giving her gums a break from wearing her dentures. She said her husband was in town and wouldn't be back for a few hours. Then, she asked if he would like to come inside for some lemonade. When she said 'lemonade,' she spread her knees apart and ran both hands under the folds of her fat and over her crotch, offering him a slice of her withered womanhood.

He quickly made some undecipherable excuse for leaving, then bolted for the sanctuary of his home. All he could think about for the next week was what Natalie would look like in her golden years. It made him shudder to think it would ever be like *that*.

Arriving at the Canfields' front door, he knocked gently three times, and listened for activity inside. After thirty seconds past, he knocked again. He wished he could just leave the casserole on the doorstep and get back home.

Bo knocked again, harder this time. The door squeaked open a couple of inches, it hadn't been closed all the way and he'd just noticed this.

Wanting to get back home as soon as possible, he stuck his head past the doorframe and called out in a gentle voice, "Hello…It's Bo from next door, hello?" He listened intently, and thought he heard a shuffling sound coming from somewhere in the back of the house.

There was a strange smell lingering in the air. He wondered if Mrs. Canfield was experimenting with Indian cooking and was using exotic curry or crushed stinkbugs for flavoring. He felt his stomach roil.

Feeling the need for a martini now more than ever, he pushed the door open and looked around, but stopped short of calling out again.

Bent over the arm of a lounge chair, Mrs. Canfield's legs and thong-draped bare ass pointed in his direction, as if waiting for a mighty stallion to mount her.

Right after he thought, *Oh God, not again.* Something unusual about her stance gave him pause. In fact, the way she was propped against the chair didn't look like a natural position at all.

"Mrs. Canfield? Are you all right?" Bo asked.

No response.

Bo stepped inside and placed the casserole on an end table in the hallway, and moved cautiously towards the old woman.

"Mrs. Canf…" He stopped about halfway from her when she came into better view. From the hips on up was missing, and a bloody trail snaked a path over the white carpet in the living room towards the kitchen. Bones with gnawed-off flesh were scattered about.

The world in Bo's head spun like the whirlpool of a flushing toilet, the aroma of fermenting sewage invading the back of his nostrils. He bent down and steadied himself on one knee.

From the hallway directly behind Bo, Mr. Canfield lumbered forth, blocking a quick exit out the front door. The old man bumped into a lamp, sending it to the floor, and alerting Bo that he wasn't alone.

When Bo first saw Mr. Canfield, he thought that the old man had thrown up blood all over the front of his pajamas, but then realized if that was true, then he had thrown up bits of his intestines, too, as there were pieces of it stuck to his pajama top. The unspeakable truth dawned on Bo then; Mr. Canfield had eaten his wife.

Mr. Canfield sauntered toward Bo like he was ready to slow dance, with his blood-stained teeth clattering like he wanted a bite to eat first.

Bo stepped backward until he felt his butt cheeks mash against Mrs. Canfield's buttocks, and found it ironic that even in death she could gross him out with her naked body.

Mr. Canfield gurgled a chilling moan of desire, and continued toward him. Finding himself between a rock and a hard place, Bo lashed out with a swift kick to Mr. Canfield's crotch, hoping to send the obviously sick man to the floor, so he could make a run for the door.

Mr. Canfield, though in his seventies, was a strong man tipping the scales at a solid two hundred and ten pounds. Bo on the other hand, was a boney one seventy-five, and just over six feet in height.

When Bo's shoe connected, he felt like he'd kicked petrified wood. Pain traveled from his big toe through his foot, up his shin, to sting like a wasp when it reached his knee.

Mr. Canfield walked into the kick like it wasn't there. Bo only had enough time to raise his left forearm in defense as blood-stained teeth tried to bite him. The sound of bone crunching cracked in the air, followed by a scream that sounded more like a woman's than a man's.

Bo felt his flesh ripping off his arm and imagined that splinters of bone left with it.

Mr. Canfield chewed on his stolen prize, looking like a mechanical corpse eating without savoring the taste. His eerie, red eyes showed no life, taking the appearance of a shark with only the primal urge to feed.

Bo wretched from the pain and from the disgusting sight of Mr. Canfield chowing down on his arm. In fear that when the old man's mouthful of meat was gone, it would be time for round two, Bo let the adrenalin take over and put every ounce of strength into his right arm.

He slammed his fist square into the left side of Mr. Canfield's jaw.

Bo watched as if in slow motion, seeing the old man's bottom jaw rip away from the skull, a wad of bloody meat flying through the air, both sets of dentures following.

That surprised Bo, he hadn't known Mr. Canfield had dentures like his wife.

With surprise now on his side, Bo dashed into the kitchen in hopes of leaving through the back door. As he turned to avoid the kitchen table, his foot slipped on a human rib marinating in a puddle of gore, and crashed full speed into the counter, right in front of a stainless steel cutlery block set.

Sensing Mr. Canfield coming from behind him, he pulled free the two largest implements from the block. One was a ten inch serrated bread knife, the other the sharpening steel.

Turning just in time to see Mr. Canfield lunge forward with his toothless upper palate, Bo thrust both weapons into the old man's eyes.

The serrated knife entered cleanly and angled upward until the end stuck out of Mr. Canfield's balding head, while the sharpening steel made a sound like the heel of a rubber boot smashing into a mud puddle.

Ooze of yellow, brown, and black splattered everywhere, some hitting Bo in the face and across his lips, causing him to gag.

Mr. Canfield fell forward, his arms going limp, and knocked Bo back against the counter, his head striking the upper cabinet, then it all went dark.

When Bo awoke, he couldn't decide what hurt worse; his left forearm or the back of his head. He felt like he was awakening from a bad dream, but it wasn't until he opened his eyes that he remembered where he was and what had happened.

As his eyes focused, he looked around frantically, expecting to see Mr. Canfield either down and out or ready to attack again. Bo was still in the Canfields' kitchen all right, but he found himself alone. No Mr. Canfield with his head now serving as a knife block. No bare assed thong wearing Mrs. Canfield. No blood, no body parts, nothing.

Bo stood and walked around in disbelief. *What the hell is going on?* he wondered.

Examining his forearm, a large chunk was missing. It wasn't bleeding or looking like he would have imagined, like the inside of a rare steak. It just looked like a mouth-sized bite was missing, looking perfectly normal except for that. It still hurt, and he wondered how he was going to explain all of this to Natalie.

After making a quick walk through each room to check for the Canfields, Bo exited the front door and went back to his house. He kept looking over his shoulder, feeling like a lion was stalking him from behind and about to overtake him at any second, until finally arriving at his door.

"Natalie, where are you? Come quick!" Bo called as he slammed the door behind him. "Natalie?"

The house was unusually silent. The kitchen was void of any of the dishes that she was preparing for Bo's brother, Miles, and his wife, Aubrey.

The lump on the back of his head began to throb.

Where's Natalie? How long have I been unconscious? he thought.

With a million questions but no answers, he searched the house without finding his wife, and returned outside to see if she was on the patio. The air outside the back of the house was stale, with no breeze blowing, and void of the smell of the roses that outlined the patio. No dogs barked, no birds sang, the wind chimes were dead silent.

Starting to feel apprehensive, he jogged to the end of his driveway and looked for any sign of life. To his delightful surprise, way down near the end of his street, he could make out his mailman, Mr. Wilkins, walking his daily route.

"Finally," Bo said aloud, and chuckled to himself for thinking for a second that everyone on Earth had vanished somehow while he was knocked out. With renewed hope, he ran down the street as fast as he could, shouting for Mr. Wilkins to stop.

Mr. Wilkins continued his route without skipping a step. Bo figured the man's hearing was waning in his old age. At first, he thought it might not be Mr. Wilkins at all, and perhaps a vacation relief in his place. But after seeing the shorts and signature white socks that came up to his knees, he knew it to be him.

"Mr. Wilkins…Damn it, man, won't you just stop? Mr. Wilkins!"

Bo couldn't believe Mr. Wilkins was ignoring him, as he was close enough now for the man to hear him.

When he was within a few feet of his mailman, Bo slowed to a fast walk, caught up to him, and placed his hand on Mr. Wilkins' shoulder.

"Mr. Wilkins, do you know what's going on around here? I…" Bo stopped cold as the man turned and met him nose to nose.

It wasn't the face of Mr. Wilkins that stared back at Bo, it was that of an emaciated face of a withered corpse under the wide brim of a postal cap. The eyes were terrifyingly red and evil, with the smile of a ghoul from his worst nightmare.

"Oh, hello, Bo. You're a welcome sight, and looking mighty fresh and tasty today. Perhaps you could spare a hand, or an entire arm, to help out your poor old mailman," Mr. Wilkins said.

Stunned, Bo couldn't believe that Mr. Wilkins had turned into whatever it was that Mr. Canfield had turned into, except Mr. Wilkins spoke rationally. That is, if asking someone for permission to eat you could be considered as rational.

"Stay back! I just want to know what's going on. Where's my wife? Where's everyone? What's happened to you?" Bo yelled, ready to hightail away if Mr. Wilkins made a move towards him.

"Oh, you know, Bo, the world is forever changing. It's important you learn to change with it," Mr. Wilkins said, dropping his mailbag from his shoulder. "If you don't, it'll eat you alive." Mr. Wilkins reached out to grab Bo with his boney fingers, but only found empty air. Bo was two steps ahead of him in anticipation and had stepped out of reach.

Unwilling to share any more body parts with the walking dead, Bo turned and ran without looking back, believing that not even the fastest cheetah in the wilds of Africa could catch him now.

With the sounds of Mr. Wilkins' snapping teeth fading in the distance, he cut between two houses and into the wooded area behind his subdivision that backed up to a county park. Without any hesitation, he climbed a six foot wire fence and snaked his way around pine, gum and water oaks. Doing his best to avoid briars and bare roots low on the ground, he pioneered a new trail running at full speed.

Having no sense of time or distance, he found himself near the edge of the woods and right behind an area of the park where locals would bring a guitar and entertain those looking to enjoy the afternoon.

A park bench was in the middle of a ten foot circle covered with limestone, reserved for the musicians. Today, there was only one person there. A short figure with broad shoulders stood with his profile to Bo as he peered at the figure through low, growing foliage. The orange glow of the setting sun behind the figure outlined a cowboy hat sitting on a skeletal rotting face, and a guitar hanging from a strap from around his neck. The skin on his naked body was so thin that Bo could count every bone.

The figure put his hand to his mouth, cleared his throat, strummed the guitar three times, and started to sing.

"The problem is all inside your head, I say to you. The answer is easy, if taken logically. I'd like to help you in your struggle, when you feed. There must be fifty ways to eat your lover. Fifty ways to eat your lover. You just start at the back, Jack. Eat the right hand, Stan. Don't forget the big toe, Bo. It's all good when you feed. Tear into that bust, Gus. You don't need to cull much. Just gnaw at the knee, Lee. It's all good when you feed."

Bo felt tiny tentacles of horror creep over his skin as the singing dead cowboy looked directly at him with his sick red eyes, as if Bo wasn't hidden in the bushes.

Before the cowboy could begin the second verse, Bo turned and ran through the woods, going back in the direction he came. Once more, he climbed the fence and followed it until coming to an access between two houses that led back to the street his house was on.

The wailing of a siren from an emergency vehicle slowly intensified. Before Bo made it to the street, an ambulance with red lights flashing zoomed past him, heading in the direction of his house.

Here was another chance that someone could give him a clue as to what was going on; a plague, a virus, or a manmade disaster. Bo chased after the speeding vehicle like a dog in pursuit of a taunting rear bumper.

The brake lights flashed and the ambulance made a quick right turn into the Canfields' driveway.

Something's wrong over there, Bo thought.

None of this was making any sense to him. He'd checked each room in the house; how did he possibly miss someone in need of medical attention? He wanted answers now, and felt he would go insane if they didn't come soon.

He reached the end of the Canfields' driveway, his chest aching from lack of breath, and stopped for a moment to rest. The throbbing in his head returned, and the bite on his forearm began to burn again in pain.

Feeling like his legs were made of lead, he plodded to the open front door of the Canfield home and saw two EMTs standing over a body. Miles and Aubrey were off to the side, holding each other, and Natalie was on her knees, sobbing next to the body.

Bo wanted to rush to Natalie, but his feet wouldn't respond. He went to call her name, but felt the power of speech forever leave him. The throbbing in his head increased so much that it clouded his vision with each beat.

Darkness colored his vision as the icy fingers of death snatched him into the next world.

"This has got to be the strangest call I've ever made. I'd like to read the police report on this one," Hector, the lead EMT said to Billy, his partner.

Billy made a face as if trying to ward off the putrid stench in the room. "They must have been starving their dog for it to do this. Looks like it ate half that old woman before it got away. I don't know what to make of the corpse with the knife in its head. And this guy," Billy nodded toward the body of Bo, lying dead on the floor. "What happened to him? I guess the dog bit him on the arm, but what killed him? The bump on his head wasn't enough to do him in. Do you think he was scared to death during the attack? A heart attack maybe?"

Hector shook his head, hoping the police would arrive soon. "They'll know more after the autopsy," he sighed, wishing he'd arrived in time to save Bo. He felt so sorry for Natalie. She'd told the two EMTs how Bo was just doing a neighborly thing and bringing over a casserole.

When Bo didn't return, she'd gone to investigate, wanting to see what was taking him so long. The casserole was still on the end table. Natalie found the Canfields' door wide open, and Bo and the others dead.

"Poor woman," Hector said about Natalie, but only loud enough for Billy to hear. He imagined how his wife would feel if she found him dead on the floor.

A faint hum emerged from Bo's throat, blending in with Natalie's sobs, until it rose loud enough in volume for her to hear.

Natalie gasped and looked at Hector. "It's Bo! He's trying to say something!"

Hector dropped to his knees beside Bo and felt for a pulse in his neck. When he felt nothing, he checked for a heart beat with his stethoscope. "I'm not getting anything. It's probably just intestinal gases working its way up through the esophagus, rattling his vocal cords."

The humming grew louder, becoming uniform and distinct.

"Wait...he's humming a tune. Listen," Billy said. Something about the hum sounded familiar. "I think I recognize it...Yeah! That's it! I know what it is! I know that song."

Billy stopped talking as Bo's piercing red eyes snapped open, seeing his world with new eyes...dead eyes.

The hope swelling in Natalie's chest that Bo was somehow still alive deflated like a balloon bursting. Bo's face contorted into unrecognizable evil, his head lunging forward to take a bite from her sweet-smelling, soft neck, with bone crushing force.

Void of any memories of the human he once was, Bo found himself compelled now only to exist to feed on the flesh of the living.

One bite at a time.

TRAPPED

P.A DOUGLAS

"How long has it really been?" He coughed viciously into his sleeve.

The continuous repetition of his coughing problem had now left a rather substantial amount of blood, mostly dried, stuck to the front of his shirt.

"How long can a man survive without sustenance?" he breathed.

Stuck, cold and alone, Vincent Carter found himself isolated within the confines of his bedroom. He had already been there for days. Or was it weeks?

He couldn't remember.

What he could remember was that he was stuck with no way out. Those *things* did a good job of reminding him of that, every day since making the decision to barricade himself within the room's four walls. At least he was locked away somewhere familiar, somewhere he could call home.

It made it easier for him to cope with the struggle at hand. Being able to skim through old photos, read old books, anything to help pass the time definitely had its part in keeping him sane so far.

The room was small, dark and cold. Even with several sheets and blankets covering him. Though fully clothed as well, Vincent was still shivering. What didn't make sense to him was the time of year. It was mid-June and he could swear the room was below sixty degrees, which was odd for Texas, to say the least.

Or was it him?

He wasn't sure.

On the walls of the room, posters hung, displaying his favorite bands and movies of the time. The picture on his nightstand; he hated looking at it. He didn't want to see her face. It made him even sicker to his stomach than he already was.

At least the bed was comfortable.

With the power off, the large flat screen television mounted to one wall did him little good. In fact, none of the electronic equipment did. His IPod stereo was out, the lights, his mini-fridge, too. It wasn't like he had anything to eat anyway; just a couple of beers, all empty now. It was useless.

He hadn't been feeling good since entering the room. After only a day or so, he'd caught a mild fever which went away shortly after. That was when the room started to change, began to get cool.

He had wedged himself into one of the corners of the room, crouched in the fetal position. The power was out so he had no idea what time it was and the boarded-up, covered windows prevented him from telling if it was night or day.

It had been like that for a while now.

Looking down at his hand, he wondered, *What if this fucking nick is what's been making me sick?*

His back had begun to cramp along with all of the other muscles in his body. Stiffening up, Vincent found it unbearable at times. Something was wrong and getting worse.

Something wet slowly dripped down from his nose to touch his lip. Whipping it away with his finger, he disregarded the yellow puss that had seeped from his nostrils, overlooking it as the fluid began to dry on the bed sheet. He couldn't see his face, because he had no mirror in the room. He however knew it was there. He could feel it with the touch. His eyes felt sunken in and wilted. They felt so tight at times it was hard to focus. His breathing began to get weak. His head throbbed with a vicious repetition, going away to come again worse than before.

Looking down at his hand and the little bit of missing flesh that revealed a bit of bone, he thought back on the things that had happened the night before.

It had taken him a while to drown out the sounds of the zombies on the other side of the door so easily. This only enforced the realization that he'd been trapped in his room for quite some time. As his eyes glazed over with deep thought, he remembered it well.

Looking back on it, had he really been prepared? Would he be in this situation at all? But then again, how could anyone prepare for something like that?

It was a rainy day and the sun was just beginning its descent. He had taken his wife of only a few months to see a movie. He couldn't recall what the movie was. It wasn't important, but what was important was the fact that on the way to the movie, an announcer said something about the dead coming to life on the radio. *Who would believe that crap?* he'd thought, assuming it was a publicity stunt for some new horror movie.

Needless to say, the odd radio messenger didn't spoil him or his wife from seeing the movie.

It was then that he noticed something strange about things other than the silly radio announcement. The movie showing was a big deal and had just come out that week, and there was hardly anyone at the theater at all. He didn't care, just glad not to have ended up dealing with the lines. He hated waiting more than anything. He was indeed an impatient man. It was one thing to wait on his lady, but standing in line for anything like buying groceries at the store or the movies was ridiculous to him. Not to mention the DMV, that place was a nightmare and he practically always refused to go there if he could afford the chance to skip out on it.

And yet, here he was going on who knows how long stuck in his room all by himself, cold, hungry and possibly even dying. It was kind of ironic really. He was running out of things to do to pass the time, which was making it harder to deal with those things outside, harder to deal with being along, and above all, harder to keep from thinking about her. It wasn't his fault what had happened. How could it be?

After the movie, he and his woman had both began to notice that things were a little different on the street, it just seemed weird and hard to place what that truly was. The movie theater wasn't the only place that seemed oddly empty. The grocery store across the street was the same way as well as the pharmacy beside that. *Where is everyone?* he wondered.

It wasn't until stopping to pump gas that the unthinkable happened. An unexpected mugger had the balls to just walk right up and attack her, right there in broad daylight. What was he supposed to do? He had her door open while he was at the pump, and the freak just jumped her. But that was just it. He wasn't just a freak, he was something else.

How could anyone be prepared for something like that?

Dashing around the car, Vincent had quickly come to his wife's aid as she screamed. When he pulled the attacker away, it was too late. The damage had been done. When he pulled the man away from the car, she was already slouched over the seat, bleeding out something awful from a neck wound, blood spurting between her fingers. There was blood everywhere. What else was he supposed to do?

It was as he pulled the man away from her, hoping someone would come and help him, that Vincent noticed it wasn't a person at all, but a creature, a zombie!

Instantly reacting as the creature leaped forward once more, Vincent threw a wild swing with his good arm. The left hand went in fast and hard, kicking the zombie in the jaw. The ghoul fell back, stumbling to the ground. It bought Vincent some time to decide what to do next.

He turned to the aid of his wife only to find that she was recovering, or at least he had thought. Staggering out of the car herself, she moaned out with wide eyes and a grimacing snarl. She was one of them!

Back in his room, Vincent snapped out of it, not wanting to remember her like that. Taking in the surroundings of his bedroom once more, he glanced down at his left hand. It was looking pretty bad. He was feeling pretty bad, restricted even. The blankets seemed to be getting tighter around him. It was hard to move. He felt ashamed for not being able to protect her.

What should I have done? he thought.

"I wish you were here," he said aloud, coughing violently into his shirt, his body wracked with pain. He was dying, he knew it. Hell, he'd seen enough horror movies to know what comes next.

It was only a matter of time and he knew it, though he didn't want to admit to himself he would be dead soon, or worse, one of *them.*

It was a miracle he'd even made it back home after the attack. Honestly, he wasn't even sure how he'd made it, but was just glad he had.

Once his wife attacked him at the gas station, Vincent had totally lost it all together. He'd shoved her away from him and then she was dead, just like that. And he had killed her.

"It was an accident! It was, it was, it was…." he screamed to the ceiling. Breaking away from the terrible memory, the guilt filling him up, Vincent broke out in tears. He hadn't meant to hurt her. It was just a little shove was all.

Once he'd pushed her away from him, she'd fallen backwards, losing her balance. She went down hard, hitting the side of her head on the base of the post right by the gas pump. When she hit, she hit so hard that he heard the dull crack of skull meeting cement. Her neck jerked wildly upon impact. The snap that sounded instantaneously sent a chill down Vincent's spine. She wasn't moving. She wasn't moving at all.

He'd knelt down to check on her to find no heartbeat or pulse. She was dead and he knew it. While his back was turned to the zombie, it began to stagger to its feet. Vincent suddenly heard the rustling from behind him. He turned to see the creature that he had momentarily put down was shambling toward him. But that wasn't what had gotten his attention. From a little farther off in the bushes, what looked like over a dozen ghouls began to pour out into the gas station parking lot. Their moans were bone chilling as they drew closer. There were over a dozen, all bearing their individual marks of death. Each mark told its story, a story of how they had died violently and no doubt painfully.

One zombie, the first in line, was missing an arm. From the outstretched limb, Vincent could see bone protruding from rotting skin and dried tissue. Its shirt was covered in blood and soaked most of the creature's pants. The same ghoul was also missing one shoe. That single foot, or the lack thereof was just pure bone scraping against cement as it dragged its leg across the pavement, leaving bits of skin behind as the foot was slowly ground down.

Another zombie in the group had at one time been a very attractive woman. Her breasts were exposed and mutilated beyond recognition. The blood and gore was horrendous. One of her hands had been gnawed down to the bone, revealing scaly fingers and yellow dripping puss. With each arm stretched out, she staggered forward with the rest of the putrid creatures.

Vincent was the only person at the gas station, something he soon realized. It was odd that the entire time he'd pumped gas he hadn't noticed this at all. The gas station was closed and the steel bars were down on the door. The street around him was empty, making the place seem like a ghost town.

Back in his bedroom, the sounds at the door suddenly got his attention, taking him out of his daydream. The ghouls were trying to get in again. He could hear them stepping slowly by the door along with thuds and bumps as fists banged on the door. With the wood nailed to the door and a dressing table in front of it, he didn't think they could get in.

"Go away! You can't get in, just go away!" he shouted from the crunched position in the corner of the room.

The banging and moaning sounds continued.

"Didn't you hear me? Go away!" Vincent breathed in heavily, hoping like hell they couldn't get in. He didn't think it was possible because it had been a while and they still hadn't managed to get in.

What he didn't understand was that even though he'd been followed home on foot by several of the ghouls, how could they have gotten into the house at all? He knew for a fact that he'd closed all the doors and locked down all the windows.

Maybe he had missed one, perhaps the back door or even the kitchen window had been left unlocked in his haste. Whatever it was that he had overlooked, it was too late now. They had made their way into the house and had tormented him day in and day out.

Trying relentlessly to get into his bedroom, the pounding would come in droves of small consistent banging. He knew they were there.

Luckily the gas station hadn't been that far from home. He didn't know why at the time, but after seeing their growing numbers and the attention he was getting, Vincent had just took off running, but not before giving one last glance at his wife.

She was gone now, and soon, he would be joining her.

It was as if his mind had just blanked out and subconsciously brought him home on its own. He was in the house before he even realized it, sobbing on the couch, crying for his sudden and unexpected loss. He called the police but the lines had been busy.

Suddenly a knocking had come at the front door. Perhaps he'd been dreaming it all, or worse, he figured and he went to see who it was. At the door, he looked out the peep hole and loathed at what he saw. A large crowd of the undead had followed him along the way. And now, they were in his front yard, trying with all they had to get in. It was a nightmare.

"Yeah, you're hungry. Go ahead, get in then, come on, break down the door!" Leaning forward in the dark room, eyes already adjusted to the gloom, he picked up the small glass partly filled with urine.

I didn't think I would ever have to resort to such tactics, but when life is at stake, people will do anything, he thought.

He had run out of water the first day into barricading himself in and had thought of his urine early on when he first began to get thirsty. It didn't taste that bad, really. It was an acquired taste to say the least, but wasn't nearly as rough as he expected.

After taking a light sip from the glass, he set it back on the bed in front of the picture on the night stand.

Suddenly, the banging at the door became more intense, more so than he had ever imagined it would get.

There must be a dozen of those things out there, he thought.

Almost instantly after hearing the sudden sounds, the door to his sanctuary crashed open, the furniture pushed aside, the wood splintering.

Two lone zombies shuffled into the exposed room with out-stretched arms and open mouths, more behind them, all pushing and shoving. Their eyes were black like tar and yellow puss leaked from them. Their jaws were dropped open, revealing blood-soaked gums and teeth. Their skin was rotting and putrid like vile from the graves of those long forgotten.

As they shuffled past the doorway toward Vincent, he noticed one of them had a bad limp and was dressed as a doctor, its once white lab coat now wrinkled and covered in dried blood. The ghoul's kneecap was exposed, revealing torn tendons and bone. Dried blood and yellow puss stained the outside edges of the wound. The creature's skin was pale like chalk. As it staggered in, it moaned with a fierce dissonance. Blood and yellow goo slid from the thing's chin, falling to the floor. The soft sound of slop splashing on the wood floor echoed in Vincent's ear. A trail of muck and gore stained the floor in the creature's wake, dripping from open sores and festering wounds.

The other zombie first through the door snarled, as they slowly got closer. Moaning in unison, the sound lightly amplified, filling the small room as more than a dozen bodies filed in.

Vincent covered his ears, trying to mute the guttural call they made. It was a useless attempt.

Another ghoul in line was a mess of blood and gore. Its scalp was torn clean off on one side, revealing the skull. The creature's cheeks were gone, torn free, the marks of teeth prevalent. All its teeth were bare. The thing had on no shirt, exposing ribs along with its entrails. A part of the zombie's chest and stomach had been ripped apart, rendering its insides visible.

The stench was overwhelming.

With them staggering in, Vincent was surprised at how calm he was. Still, he clung tightly to his blankets as he huddled in the corner, too afraid and weak to react. He just sat there quivering, and waiting for them to reach him. He was too dehydrated and malnourished to defend himself. It had just been too long, stuck in his room with nothing to eat or drink.

"Do your worst, you rotting piles of filth! Come and get me! You know you want what I've got! I hope you rot in Hell!" He leaned forward and spit at the first two creatures closing in, but only blood came out of his mouth.

Instantly following the yelling endeavor, a furious cough caught in his throat, sending him into a violent fit, as blood spilled into his lap. It soaked into the blankets wrapped around him. The acidic liquid was a mixture of dark reds and yellows.

"Bastards!" he yelled at the creatures in mock triumph, instantly bursting into a hysterical laughter. "I'm dead anyway!"

The first two zombies finally reached him. With mouths open wide and eyes even wider, the two ghouls drooled with anticipation. Vincent squirmed about, but to no avail as the dead closed in, hungry for his flesh.

Closing his eyes tight with fear, he knew his fate. It was time. He just hoped like hell that it wasn't going to hurt.

Of course it was going to hurt. Who was he kidding?

Gnashing and clawing of teeth into skin, then red and white flesh, then bone.

Deeper and deeper.

"Noooo." He let out a light whimper, trying his best to pull the blankets up over his head, as if in one last attempt at getting away from what was to come.

The first one was touching him. He could feel the cold hands all over him. The foul breath, the smell, it was all over him.

Time slowed down as he felt its teeth sink into his arm, another zombie biting into his right leg, while another bent down to feed on his left one. The pain was sharp and instant. Then it came, wetness and warmth.

Another creature darted in, teeth sinking into his jugular. Pulling away furiously and with malice, the zombie tore Vincent's throat open. Blood and bubbles poured out as he tried to scream.

Instantly he felt another one grab him by the arms, pulling at him, restricting him.

Falling to his side on the bed, Vincent bled out violently while being devoured helplessly by the festering, rotting ghouls.

One of the last things he heard before the life finally drained from his body was the slurping and chomping of his demise. The feast was in full swing.

Outside the room Vincent was in, two people stood talking before a two way mirror, watching Vincent battle his inner demons.

"How long has he been like this, Doctor?" the intern asked.

"Almost all of his life, believe it or not," the doctor replied. "It's sad really."

"Do we know the cause of his symptoms?" the second doctor jotted down a few notes. "I've never seen anyone so delusional."

"Yes, I know. This is undoubtedly the worst case of paranoid schizophrenia I've ever come across. I was recently assigned to his case and can't seem to quite put my finger on it. He seems to be suffering from mass delusions of some kind. Either my nursing assistant or myself have been administering his medication via syringe for the last two years and…"

"Why is that?"

"Why what, exactly? If you're asking about our method of administering the medication, he refuses to take it."

"Not to get off subject, but how's that knee of yours doing? I couldn't help but notice it's been bothering you lately," the intern asked.

BONE CLEANERS

KATIE SIMMONS

Dave Garner lay peacefully sleeping under his crisp clean sheets. The comforter his wife picked out was so billowy and white all that stuck out from underneath it was his head, and he looked like a tiny man being squished by a mass accumulation of clouds.

He was in the midst of enjoying a heavenly dream when he was awakened by the ear-piercing, torturing screech of his alarm clock.

"Ugh," he grunted as he swung his arm around to slam his palm down on the **OFF** button. "I need to find another job."

Dave wasn't a morning person. Waking up any time before nine a.m. was considered inhumane, so really he was pretty much limited to the jobs he could take. Currently he was employed as a postal worker and in general he didn't mind his job. He liked telling dirty and inappropriate jokes to the younger people working at the various stops along his route, he liked the pleasant friendly chats with the older folks, but he hated waking up at what he considered to be the crack of dawn. If he could stomach the sweltering humid days of summer, the vicious attacks from unchained dogs, and the lazy neighbors who didn't shovel their sidewalks in the winter, he considered it a good day.

As he sat on the corner of his bed in his white and blue-striped boxers and white cotton t-shirt, he rubbed his eyes and let out a long and powerful yawn. To make the mornings bearable, he organized them very precisely so he could make them productive rather than having them turn into the tedious and monotonous task of getting ready for work that they truly were.

His wife knew he had trouble getting motivated in the morning, so she had the not so bright idea of painting everything white. She said it was too make him cheery and feel awake in the morning, but he hated it. He felt like he was living in an asylum, while other mornings, he felt like he was part of a science experiment. White is okay, but not in every single room and every piece of furniture; it was nauseating.

He groggily made his way to the master bathroom and turned on the bright light, which triggered the chain reaction of his eyes wanting to revert back to sleep mode. This was actually not another one of his wife's ploys to help wake him up in the mornings. He actually liked the bathroom being bright and spotless.

He was extremely anal when it came to having a clean mirror and sink that he could shave at. He shaved every morning even when he didn't need to and always finished it off with his expensive bottle of imported French aftershave.

After he finished the shave and lathering his smooth face with the intoxicating aroma, he rinsed off his razor, and dried it off so it wouldn't rust.

He then placed it in the felt-lined case and placed it back into the cabinet in its little nook. He then turned off the light and walked over to the bed to put on his slippers.

He looked at his wife who was still sleeping. It was funny how she had to leave for work at nearly the same time as he did, but she slept in until moments before she had to leave. To him that was crazy, chaotic.

He liked to be able to roam around and relax in the morning, he hated to rush. Rushing in the morning to get to work made it seem all the more forced. He liked going at his own pace; that way going to work seemed more like an option, where as rushing because you're going to be late only proves the point that you have no choice but to go.

Dave pattered across the freshly-cleaned, shiny wooden floor of the bedroom, the only thing in the room that wasn't white. He opened the door and went into the living room where his white Pomeranian was sleeping.

His friends made fun of him endlessly for having such a small powder puff dog, but they knew it fit him. A man who was as organized and anal about things as Dave was would not have an oversized slobbering hound. The petite, pristine white pup served his need for a friendly companion when his wife would give him the cold shoulder. He gave the dog the fitting name of Lilly to represent her clean white appearance.

Dave picked up Lilly's leash and hooked it on to her tiny lavender collar. Lilly yawned as she stretched out her small, fluffy fur-covered legs and let out a meek little yawn. Dave scooped her up in his arms and went to the front living room window. He stood for a good five minutes, staring out from behind the sheer white curtains, looking for the right time to take her out to do her business. He could hear his wife rustling in the bedroom and looked back to see her walking towards him to join him at the front window.

"Why don't you just take her out already?" she asked, questioning his cautious behavior.

"I want to make sure he's not out there," Dave replied.

"David," she began in an irritated tone. "Mr. Pitman is not going to be out there this early."

"I wouldn't be so sure of that," Dave scoffed. "And I'm not taking the chance."

"So, what are you going to do?" She headed over to the kitchen to start a pot of coffee. "Are you going to stand there all morning till she pees on you?"

"No, Darla," he said, only paying her half a mind as he focused on his neighbor's house.

Darla shook her head. "I don't know why you hate that man so much?" she stated.

"Is that supposed to be a trick question?" he asked. "If it is, I have a better one. What's there to like about him?" he asked with a scoff, understanding the mean and hideous nature of his elderly neighbor. "I thought seniors were supposed to be nice," he said below his breath.

"Most of them are," Darla chimed in over the slow gurgle of the coffee maker. Most of them are in fact incredibly nice, it's almost unbelievable," she stated.

"Well, you would know," he replied. "You work with them everyday."

"That's right I do. That's how I know you shouldn't judge Mr. Pitman. He may be unpleasant because of a serious problem."

"He is the problem," Dave scoffed under his breath.

"Just go," she said. "You can't do this everyday as long as he's our neighbor."

Dave shot her an irritated glance. She had no idea how horrible Mr. Pitman was. "Oh yeah?" he asked. "Is that why we had to hire someone to come cut our front lawn? Both of us can't stand to come in contact with him. Even you keep your car tucked away in the garage every morning until the door is all the way open so you can peel out in a fast getaway. After work it's the same thing. You even got a stronger remote garage opener so you can open the door before you even get near our house. Then one day you almost took our mail box out because you pulled into the driveway so fast."

Darla laughed. "That's right. That was pretty funny," she said with a smile. "You should have seen your face."

"Yes. Very funny," he said, not amused. "It's a shame I have to deliver his mail. Which according to him I can't even do right," he grumbled.

"Well, he's old. He's set in his ways," Darla said as if she were defending him.

"How many ways is there to receive your mail?" he exclaimed. "It's clean, it's intact, it's all there and it's unopened. What does he want?"

"I guess he's just a little anal."

"Oh, no," he argued, shaking his head.

"Oh, I'm sorry. You would know." Darla was poking fun at him.

"No. I'm not anal," he said mockingly. "I am organized, and clean." He pointed to Mr. Pitman's house. "That man is none of those things. He just thinks he has power and pushes other people around."

"Well…" she said as she motioned towards Dave huddled at the corner of the window like a scared child. "He seems to have some power over you."

"He doesn't have power over me," Dave replied angrily. "He has the power of stench!"

"Stench?" Darla asked.

"Yes. You never got close enough to him to see his true ugliness. You know that dingy green robe he's always wearing? Well, it smells wretched. His hair, which is always greasy, smells like rotting bacon, which can only tell me he cooks a lot of bacon and never takes a shower. His breath…" He continued in a musical fashion "Oh my God, his breath, and the crusty sleepers that are always in his eyes, oh, and his nose hairs!" Dave had to stop going on about Mr. Pitman and his numerous foul characteristics as he was on the verge of gagging.

Darla just looked at him with a strange look.

"Don't look at me like that, Darla. I realize I only named his physical characteristics, but that's only because his mannerisms and etiquette while dealing with people are far worse."

She just shook her head and poured herself a cup of coffee. "I'm going to drink my coffee and get ready, and you can stand there all morning if you want. If you ask me, now would be your best chance to take Lilly out before Mr. Pitman has a chance to spot you."

Dave sighed and let go of the curtain. He walked over to the door, cursing the steep hill in the back which made Lilly going in the backyard impossible, therefore forcing him to take her into the front yard to do her business.

He repositioned Lilly and placed her in his left arm. He reached out for the door knob and quickly turned it, realizing it would make the least noise, than if he slowly turned it allowing it to grind and echo across the early morning silence. When the door was cracked open, he glanced over into Mr. Pitman's yard.

Mr. Pitman's house was set further back than his was so Dave wasn't able to see onto his front porch. When Dave believed it was safe for him and Lilly to venture outside, he stepped one foot onto the porch mat, followed by the other, then took off down the steps, leaving the door open for a quick escape back inside.

He dropped Lilly in the yard in hopes she would go right away, her tiny body nearly getting lost in the tall uncut grass.

As Dave stood hunched down low to the ground in hopes of hiding himself from Mr. Pitman's front window, he suddenly stood up straight like someone had taken a 4x4 to his lower back, as he heard Mr. Pitman call out to him. "You keep an eye on that shit machine of yours!" the man yelled.

Dave winced and slowly turned to face Mr. Pitman, who was making his way down his front steps. "Good morning, Mr. Pitman!" Dave called out with a friendly wave.

"There's nothing good about it!" Mr. Pitman exclaimed as he made his way closer to Dave and Lilly, cutting across his front lawn. "There was nothing good about last evening either when I nearly broke my back while trying to shovel a heap of dog crap the size of Rhode Island out of my yard."

Dave backed away when he saw Mr. Pitman getting closer.

Mr. Pitman pointed down at Lilly, who was staring up at him and growling. "I hope you don't intend for that to happen again," he said in a threatening manner.

Dave was taken aback by the assumption. "You think it was my dog that did it?" he said with a laugh. "Why, she only does her business on this side of the yard, far away from yours, and you know it can't possibly be as big as Rhode Island, be serious."

"I am serious," Mr. Pitman said. "Keep your dog and its feces off my lawn."

Dave looked at him with a smirk. "I will when you keep yourself off my lawn," he said rather proud of himself, noticing Mr. Pitman was in Dave's yard now.

Mr. Pitman glared at him angrily and got right in his face. "The day you see me taking a squat on your front lawn, then you can say that to me, David!" he exclaimed.

Dave relaxed with a deep breath as Mr. Pitman turned away to go back to his house, but tensed up again when the old man turned around for one last attack.

"I expect my mail on time this morning, too."

Dave shook his head. "I can deliver it on time this afternoon, but not in the morning, you know that, Mr. Pitman. This part of my route isn't till after lunch."

"Well, then change it!" he exclaimed bitterly as he let spit fly into Dave's face.

Dave gagged and wiped his face off. Mr. Pitman remained standing on Dave's lawn, staring at him as he ran up his front steps and slammed the front door behind him.

"Ahhhhh, that man!" Dave screamed as he dropped Lilly on the living room floor and ran to the kitchen sink.

"What's the matter?" Darla shouted as she came running out of the bathroom, fully-dressed and her makeup half on.

"He sprayed me!" Dave sputtered as he began to fill his hands with the running water.

"With what?" she asked upon seeing he was splashing his face with water.

"With his toxic spit!" Dave groaned as he reached for the soap. "Ah, forget it," he sighed. "I'll just take a shower."

Darla went back into the room to finish her makeup while Dave went to go hop in the shower.

As Dave soaped up his hair, he hollered out to Darla in desperation, "We have to get a fence put up or something! His attacks went from being verbal, to being physically threatening to my own persona hygiene!"

"Oh, for heaven's sake," Darla grumbled. "You can be such a pansy!"

Dave dismissed the comment as he lathered himself up with soap and rinsed off. When finished, he wrapped himself in a towel and pushed the shower curtain aside.

Darla came in and smiled. "I guess you're going to put on a fresh layer of aftershave," she teased.

He looked at himself in the mirror. "That's a good idea! Perhaps the alcohol in it will kill any bacteria that the soap didn't take care of."

She shook her head and kissed him quickly. "See you later, honey, love you."

Dave kissed her back and returned the pleasantries. "Love you too, babe," he said with a smile as he watched her walk out the door.

He opened up the medicine cabinet to splash on some fresh aftershave. "Pansy," he mumbled. "Where'd she ever get that idea?"

He made his way into the bedroom where his work uniform was laid out on the bed, crisp and clean like he made sure of every morning. All the other workers didn't take much pride in the appearance of the uniforms; they said if they were going to get dirty anyway, and wrinkled underneath the heavy mail bag, then what was the point? Dave on the other hand always paid mind to his appearance, making sure it was always at its best.

After he was dressed, he went into the living room, popped on the news and headed into the kitchen to have a bowl of cereal. As he poured the cold milk over the frosty flakes overflowing in his bowl, he could hear the news softly mumbling in the background, though he couldn't make out the reports.

He never watched the news or really cared what was going on. He always figured if something really bad was happening, he would find out the really important stuff once he got to work.

Dave arrived at work about twenty minutes early and went into the break room kitchen to grab a cup of coffee. When he had his cup of coffee, he walked into the employee lounge where he planned on sitting down and chatting with some of the guys. However, when he got there, he saw everyone standing around the television in silence.

"What's going on?" he asked.

"Don't you know?" Donna asked. She was a middle-aged mother of two with brown hair and wide hips. "It's been all over the news this morning."

"I don't watch the news," Dave replied as he tried looking through the crowd of people to see the television.

"Well, you should have been watching this morning," she said. "There was an explosion at one of the military stations about fifty miles west of here. Authorities are saying it was a site that was forced to get rid of its nuclear arms and some were said to be experimental. While in transport, one of the trucks got into an accident and the radiation began to seep out into the air. Thankfully no one was hurt. The men transporting the weapons had on their radiation suits, but the problem is still out there. Now there's radiation floating into the atmosphere and surrounding area."

"That's terrible," Dave said as he watched the pictures flash by on the screen. He was still enthralled in the news story when the manager came storming in.

"All right, listen up, people," he said. "I know you're all worried about what just happened, but it doesn't affect any of us. It's work as usual. If, and I mean 'if' anything changes, you all have your cell phones with you. We'll send out a mass message telling you what you're to do if the situation worsens. Now, get out there and deliver the mail!"

Dave watched at how quickly the manager disappeared through the door again.

"Ha!" Antonio scoffed, a young Italian man in his early twenties, with dark black hair and a perpetual tan. He always talked with his hands. "Of course he's not worried, he gets to sit in here all day."

"I wouldn't worry about it," Dave said. "After all, the news is just reporting it; it's not saying anything like 'stay indoors and seal up your windows, there's radiation coming your way'!"

"Oh shut up, Dave," Antonio groaned. "You just want to make sure your grumpy old neighbor gets his mail so he doesn't chew your ass out."

"Damned right," Dave agreed. "Right now that's the biggest fear I have, facing that man is like a bull fight. The thing on the other end is vicious, stubborn and keeps coming at you."

Antonio shook his head and went to go collect his mail bag, Dave following.

Dave started to sort through all his mail, getting it ready for his route. He made sure Mr. Pitman's mail was separated and well taken care of. The route past Mr. Pitman's house wasn't until after lunch, but Dave wanted the man's mail with him, where he could keep any eye on it at all times.

Dave went out to his mail truck, climbed in, drove to the dock where he loaded the mail bins into the back, and drove over to where he began his route. Then he started his first rounds of the morning.

Two hours later he was doing fine and right on time. So far, the morning was going good, but he figured that was because he was on the good half of his day. The sun was shining bright and the air was a warm seventy-two degrees.

Perfect, he thought. The first fifty or so houses always proved to be the toughest because his mail bag was so heavy, but later in the shift his bag became lighter and the pain in his shoulder would always begin to fade away. When eleven o' clock hit, he was hungry. He was finishing up the rest of the houses on his route when he looked up at the sky and noticed strange, dark clouds approaching from the west.

"That's weird," he said aloud to himself.

The clouds were a deep almost purplish color, nothing like he had ever seen before. He figured he better hurry with this route and get back to the office.

As he drove back for lunch, he kept an eye on the sky. As the clouds approached, he could see they were spreading out much further than he thought. An uneasy feeling came over him when he noticed there were far less cars on the road than usual. He then looked down at his cell phone on the seat next to him, expecting it to ring, but it never did. He figured if it was something serious, he would have gotten a call to head back to the office.

Dave reached the office just as the thunder started to rumble in the distance and the wind began to pick up. He quickly parked his mail truck out back with all the others and locked it while he headed in for lunch.

When he reached the break room, it was like déjà vu. There was a group of people gathered around the television again, but this time there were more of them. He also noticed many others there as well, talking on their cell phones, and some just lounging around with their feet resting on the small coffee table.

"What's going on?" he asked Antonio.

"Those storm clouds out there; they may be bringing the radiation our way. We have to stay here until the storm blows over," Antonio replied.

"And maybe even overnight," Maria said angrily as she walked by. She was in her late sixties and had been employed with the postal service for over thirty years.

"What?" Dave exclaimed. "How come no one called me?"

Antonio looked down at Dave's cell phone in his hand and sighed. He grabbed it and shoved it in Dave's face. "How come you have your phone turned off, stupid?"

"Oh," Dave said quietly as he felt his face grow red from embarrassment. He took the phone from Antonio and went to go sit down in a chair in the corner of the room. He flipped the phone open and turned it on. A minute later he saw he had ten missed calls and two new messages. After listening to the messages, he was happy to see that one was from work; they hadn't forgotten about him.

The other message was from Darla and he was relieved to hear she was safe. She was spending the night at work and told him he should do the same. No one knew if the rain was going to bring the radiation but no one wanted to venture outside to find out, either.

With nothing else to do, Dave and the others got comfortable for the long wait.

By the time the rain stopped it was already eight o' clock. It had rained hard and lightly all afternoon and evening, but never fully stopped for anyone to go outside. Everyone decided to call it an early night.

No one knew what was ahead of them tomorrow and none of them knew if they would be able to sleep. Either they would be too worried or too uncomfortable. Dave, of course, was both. He was worried about Mr. Pitman not getting his mail, he was worried about Darla being alone at work, he was worried about his sweet little Lilly, home all alone with an angry neighbor to contend with, and he was worried he wouldn't get any sleep curled up in the uncomfortable leather chair he'd chosen to sleep in.

It wasn't until sometime around five a.m., when Dave believed he managed to fall asleep, but it didn't matter, he was soon awakened at eight by someone turning on the television to watch the news.

The hum of the TV began to wake people up one by one. Everyone groaned and stretched as they tried to tweak the pain from their bodies after spending the night sleeping on the cold floor or a chair too small for their bodies.

But soon, they all stood in front of the television, eager to hear what the verdict was.

"Maria!" Dave called out from the coffee machine. "Can you turn it up?"

Maria adjusted the volume so Dave could hear and he began to listen as the newscaster started to spill out their fate.

"The horrible incident that occurred around five yesterday morning didn't take any lives, thankfully, but it did force thousands of scared people into their homes when rain clouds moved in. The rain has long since stopped, but people are still wondering if it's safe to go outside." The female newscaster stopped talking and turned it over to a fellow newsman.

"Thank you, Trisha," the newsman said. "I'm Mike Roberts and yes," he began, "here is the answer everyone's been waiting for. The authorities have had scientists outside with Geiger counters to see if the air has harmful radiation in it. The answer is no. The fifteen mile radius surrounding the incident was affected by the rain, but the rain that permeated outside that area was safe. It's now safe to go about your daily business. Let's be thankful we were able to escape what could have been a very bad situation." He shifted position and behind him a sports logo appeared on his green screen. "In other news, the team…"

Maria turned off the television as the anchorman began to talk about other news no one was really interested in.

"Well, you heard them, people!" the manager shouted. "It's business as usual. I'll give everyone an extra hour to get to their routes, basically just finish up the routes you had from yesterday and head home. I'll see you all tomorrow when we're back to normal business."

Everyone left and went their separate ways.

Dave sat down to finish his coffee; he was in no rush to deliver Mr. Pitman's mail. He was already a day late in getting it to him, so another hour couldn't possibly make the grouchy old man's attitude worse. Dave also was worried about his girls, Darla and Lilly. He picked up his cell phone and called Darla's work, but when the receptionist answered, she told him Darla had already gone home.

He was relieved. He was worried that the rain may have been worse her way as she was only about thirteen or so miles outside of the fifteen mile radius and he wasn't sure he believed the whole *the air is safe* bit.

Dave noticed George, his crazy conspiracy theory obsessed co-worker, walking out the door in a hurry. He carried with him his postal bag full of yesterday's mail and a huge duffel bag that looked pretty heavy.

"Do you believe what they were saying on the news?" Dave asked him as he walked by.

"Hell no!" George exclaimed in a gruff voice. "Anytime something like this happens, shit follows. The news isn't gonna tell you right off the bat. Either they don't know or they don't want to cause a panic. It's out there all right." He stared eerily out the window.

"What is?" Dave asked as, he too, glanced out the window George was gazing through.

"I don't know yet, Dave," George said in a stoic fashion. "However, my son and I are getting ready for it." He motioned down to his duffel bag as he dropped it on the floor. "There's enough firearms and ammo in here to take on five military units or more."

Dave chuckled, but fearing George's crazy temper, he kept it to himself. Besides, he didn't want to think why George had so many guns with him at work. Images of the man 'going postal' came to mind and Dave shuddered. "I don't think we have to fear the army, George," Dave said. "It was all a mistake with something they were trying to get rid of. When it happened they tried fixing it right away."

"I don't buy it," George growled. "Anyways, it's not the Army I'm afraid of; it's what's going to follow the radiation. It's never good I can tell you that much."

Dave just looked away and wondered if George's conspiracy theory had a point.

"Well," George said as he picked up his duffel bag. "Best of luck to you, with whatever ends up happening."

"Thanks," Dave said as George headed out the door in a determined fashion.

Dave got up from his chair and threw away his paper coffee cup when Antonio followed him over to the garbage can. "What was George going on about?" he asked.

"Oh," Dave sighed. "Don't worry about him, be glad he's leaving. He's just paranoid."

"Yeah, aren't we all," Antonio scoffed as he turned to walk away.

"What do you mean?" Dave asked before Antonio had left.

"George has a point, you know. This has bad news written all over it," Antonio said. "I'm getting my route done and going home. I hope to see you tomorrow, man."

Dave nodded as Antonio exited the door.

"Man," Dave sighed to himself. "I need to find a different job. These people around here are nuts."

Maria walked by and chuckled, "Who are you calling a nut? Go look at yourself in the mirror, you look like crap."

Dave reached up and felt the stubble on his chin. He groaned, knowing that was going to bug him all day. He wanted badly to go home and shave but he figured the sooner he got done with his route the sooner he could get home and spend the rest of the day relaxing with his wife and dog.

Dave punched back in with his time card and headed out to his mail truck. As he walked through the parking lot, he noticed there were only about five people who still had to leave.

Good, he thought. *I'm not the last one leave the office.*

He sighed deeply while trying to catch his breath. The moisture was still heavy in the air, and the early morning sun was already making it humid and unbearable.

He heaved his mail bag into his truck and tossed it on the floor next to him. When he got into his seat, he bent down to check to make sure Mr. Pitman's mail was still there. When he saw it was safe in its usual place, he started up his truck and sat straight up. He caught a glimpse of himself in the mirror and gasped. "Oh God, I do look like crap." He felt the stubble on his face and noticed his disheveled hair and baggy eyes. *You sure can tell I didn't get much sleep last night,* he thought as he observed the puffy-sick look of his eyes.

He sighed once more and drove away, ready to start his mail route.

When Dave approached Walnut Street, he could see another mail truck off to the side of the road. It looked like it was Antonio's — cause of the small dent on the passenger side — but as Dave drove by, he realized it wasn't parked; it was *crashed* into a tree on the sidewalk and Antonio was nowhere to be found.

He grabbed his cell phone and dialed the station. "Anyone hear from Antonio?" he asked the manager.

The only response he received was, "No, I haven't heard from him since he left this morning."

Dave found it strange but decided to continue on after reporting the condition of Antonio's mail truck. Let the manager handle it. He wasn't about to go combing the streets for someone who may not even be around. Knowing Antonio, he probably crashed his truck on purpose so he could head home early. It wouldn't be the first time he had an 'accident' so he could get off work.

Dave continued on until he saw a car in the same situation. He stopped behind the vehicle and got out. As he walked closer, he could see the side windows were broken, and steam was coming from the hood. It was empty but there was blood splattered on the front seat.

"What's going on around here?" he asked himself as he looked around to see a rather desolate street, which was strange in itself. This time of day there should have been people walking dogs, cars driving by, and people in their yards, gardening or playing with toddlers too young to go to school yet.

He ran back to his truck and locked the door in a panic. It was just too creepy for him.

He made his first stop nearly running to the front door. When he got there, he could see the door was cracked open.

That's strange, he thought. He went to the next house and could see that the front windows were broken and the curtains were blowing in the wind through the broken glass. He began to panic. He ran to the next house, dropped the mail in the box, rang the door bell to be polite, and ran.

He did this to the next five houses in a row, and was shocked to see that when he looked back down the street at the homes, no one had come out. Even the few that were waiting on welfare or social security checks. Normally, they were on him before he reached their porch.

These were all houses which he knew were homes of those who stayed home during the day. No one was on the street and there wasn't a sound anywhere except for the wind. He ran back to his truck and decided to do the rest of his route with the truck as close to him as possible.

This was rather easy for him because with exception of his own street, the rest of his route consisted of mailboxes at the edge of the curb which allowed him to just stick his arm out the window as he drove by and drop it into the boxes.

When he finally reached his own street, the last street on his route, he had to get out and walk, and he cursed the builders of the houses for not putting the mailboxes on the curb like the other homes.

After he completed all the houses on his street, he decided to park his truck in front of his driveway and just walk over to Mr. Pitman's, then he would be able to go back to the office and get his car and go home for the day.

As he held the mail in his hands for both his house and Mr. Pitman's, he made his way up the old man's sidewalk. He strolled towards Mr. Pitman's porch in a quick but silent fashion.

Dave was already a nervous wreck about how Mr. Pitman would react in receiving his mail a day late, plus all the other weird occurrences that had happened. After finding Antonio's empty mail truck, a wrecked car with broken windows and blood on the front seat, and rows of empty houses with busted out windows, it only added to the eerie feeling. He wanted to give Mr. Pitman's his mail and run home to check on his wife and dog.

Dave made it safely to Mr. Pitman's front porch without being seen by the old man. He dropped the letters in the mail box and leaped back off the porch steps, landing on the front lawn. But he didn't make it three steps before he could see Mr. Pitman a good ten feet away from him, walking slowly in his direction as he came around from the backyard. He'd heard Dave pull up in the mail truck.

Dave kept his eyes straight ahead as he began to attempt to smooth talk the old man. He knew to make eye contact would get the man going. It had in the past.

"Now, Mr. Pitman, I apologize about the delay with your mail, but I'm sure you've watched the news and know what's been going on."

Dave got no response as Mr. Pitman got closer.

"So," Dave continued, nervously still staring straight ahead. "We were told to stay in work until the rain passed and it was proven to be safe out here. So, you see, Mr. Pitman, I was forbidden to leave work and deliver your mail, but I did so this morning as promised."

At this point Dave could see Mr. Pitman stopped walking towards him but that was only because he was right on top of him now. Dave grew motionless when he could smell the old man's rank breath blowing down upon him. Dave cringed, wondering why the man could never brush his teeth, but this time he noticed the smell was even more wretched than usual. It was something that he couldn't even attempt to identify; he just knew it was gut-wrenching nastiness.

Dave just stood there, remaining still, as he waited for Mr. Pitman to finally start in on his verbal assault. But much to Dave's surprise, the old man didn't say a word.

Then Dave's blood ran cold when he heard a low, continuous moan coming from Mr. Pitman.

Dave turned slowly and stared right into then man's pale, rotting face. He let out a terrified scream as Mr. Pitman glared at him with sunken dead eyes. His flesh, which had always been old and saggy, was now a mottled gray, shiny and nearly sliding off his bones! Underneath the skin of his face where it seemed to have lost its grip on the cheek bones, Dave could see the inner workings of Mr. Pitman's face. His lips seemed to have disappeared and any other part of skin on his face and neck seemed to be rotting away before his very eyes.

Dave backed away as Mr. Pitman opened his mouth wide and appeared as if he was going to take a bite out of him. Dave gave him a quick and powerful kick to the gut, which sent the old man falling onto the ground.

Dave turned and ran for his house. When he reached his front door and dropped his mail on his doorstep, he began fumbling with his keys. Just as he was turning the doorknob, he looked over to see Mr. Pitman slowly getting up from the ground and making his way across the lawn in a very animated, yet lethargic way.

Dave quickly opened the door and fell inside his living room. He shut the front door and bolted it quickly. He crawled over to his couch and sank into its billowy cushions. He hated to say it but it appeared as if Mr. Pitman had turned into some kind of zombie.

"But how?" he wondered aloud to himself. "That's impossible."

Dave automatically turned his attention to the TV, as if it was calling out to him. He flipped on the news and began to watch in horror as a living nightmare unfolded before him. Everything in his present environment seemed to turn into a blur around him as he focused all his attention on the news.

"Now you see it, folks," the newsman reported as a clip of a graveyard popped up on the screen. "As amazing as it sounds, throngs of dead people seemed to have unearthed themselves and are now roaming the streets."

Dave stared in horror as he watched the ground of several graves turn upward as the dead began to free themselves from their underground prisons.

Dave turned his attention back to the newsman as the video left the graveyard and went back to the studio. "General opinion on the cause of this apocalyptic type event is that the radiation that rained down on the Earth sank into the ground and infected the bodies of the corpses, giving them new life. We've all seen this in movies, television shows, and have read about it in books. And why? Perhaps because it was all made up; we believed it could never happen. Well, I'll tell you this: it has happened. The only question now is: are we going to let it continue?"

Dave listened in awe and he started to crawl closer to the television screen as a newswoman took over. "Police and other government officials are asking everyone to stay in their homes. There is no word on how dangerous, fast or intelligent these walking dead creatures are but we encourage everyone to stay indoors. We know how it spreads, so keep yourself safe, don't let them get to you, and it should eventually die out."

The newsman laughed nervously. "Agreed. People, stay inside. If you have to get to loved ones, don't leave home empty handed. If you have a gun that's probably your best bet, otherwise grabbing the sharpest or bluntest object you can find will work just as well. The further you stay away from them the better. Just consider yourself lucky we found this from the start; we have a chance to stop it. The authorities are even now…"

Dave turned off the television and nearly had a heart attack when he saw a reflection in the TV of a figure standing behind him. He turned around and let out a sigh of relief when he saw it was Darla with Lilly in her arms.

"What's wrong?" she asked almost in shock.

Dave ran over and hugged her. They stayed that way until they were both startled by garbage cans getting knocked over in the driveway.

"Oh my God," Darla gasped when she saw Mr. Pitman staring in the front window at them, blood dripping from his teeth. "He must have attacked someone," she said.

Dave, suddenly feeling a burst of adrenaline and power, ran down into the basement and emerged a minute later with an axe and a softball bat.

He held them both and asked, "Which one do you want?"

Darla sighed, not wanting to answer, but realizing it wasn't an option to back out, she chose the softball bat.

Dave dashed to the front door, axe in hand, and motioned for Darla to stay inside. He stepped out onto the front porch like a gunslinger ready for a duel. He stood his ground, the axe gripped tightly in hand, as Mr. Pitman turned to face him.

He believed that even though the toxic walking dead had turned Mr. Pitman into one of them, Dave could swear the old man still knew what was going on. Dave felt that even though Mr. Pitman was standing there with his flesh rotting from his very bones, and his brain dead from the virus, the grouchy neighbor still had a recollection that he hated Dave.

Not having a problem with what he knew he had to do, as Dave had wanted to kill Mr. Pitman for a long time, and since in a sense Mr. Pitman was already dead, he welcomed the opportunity.

Mr. Pitman suddenly lunged forward and ran at him. Dave brought back the axe and gave a wide, heavy swing. The axe came down and sliced right down the center of Mr. Pitman's skull. He turned his face away as Mr. Pitman's head separated and blood and brain matter went splashing through the air, splattering against Dave's clean, white, perfect house.

Dave stood triumphantly covered in Mr. Pitman's blood, with even more of it dripping from the axe blade which he heroically rested on his shoulder. At that moment Dave felt alive, and for the first time ever he felt like he had the courage to throw away the safe, organized life he had and cause chaos to the throngs of undead that were sure to be heading his way.

He headed back inside, to which Darla gasped at his appearance. "You want to go change?" she asked.

"No. There would be no sense in that," he said with a grin that showed trouble.

"Why's that?" Darla asked, afraid to hear the answer.

"We're going out there," he replied.

"Are you crazy?" she exclaimed. "There are more of them out there."

"I know," he replied calmly. "That's why we're going out there. If this is like in the movies, then if we wait around in here, that'll only provide them with an opportunity to grow in numbers. They gather where there are other humans. If we get them now, chances are we can knock them out one at a time before they unite and turn into a sea of bone cleaners."

"Bone cleaners?" Darla asked as she shook her head, not sure if she heard him correctly.

"That's right," he said. "Think about it."

"I thought they eat brains?"

"Brains, flesh, whatever that's alive really," he replied as if he was a master on the subject.

"Then why is it in movies that people turn into them and aren't skeletons?"

"Well," he began to explain. "If you managed to sit through a zombie movie with me once in your life you would have noticed that there are three possible options/outcomes. The first is that you kill the zombie, and 'boom' you're in luck and you're safe for the time being. Second option is you get bit and are quick enough to get away, but sorry, you'll soon become one of them. The third option is you get bit, and you are either too slow to get away or you get overtaken so you're pretty much dinner for a group of zombies that are going to enjoy the entire piece of you right down to the bone."

"Great," Darla said. "So, three out of three, we're screwed."

"Not yet we're not." He looked at Lilly, who was still sitting patiently in Darla's arms. He went to the closet and took out a backpack. Darla watched with a smile on her face, trying to hold back her laughter as she watched Dave carefully place Lilly in the small backpack, tie it securely so only the dog's fluffy head was sticking out, then strap it to his back.

He looked at her resentfully when he heard her chuckle. "What?" he asked angrily. "I don't think she would be able to handle the chainsaw in the basement, and I'm not going to have her eaten by those things."

Darla picked up the keys for the mail truck and they headed out the front door with weapons in hand. When they got outside, they saw a pickup truck speed away with people waving from the rear bed. "Thanks for the gas!" they shouted as the vehicle sped down the street.

"Wait!" Dave exclaimed. He and Darla ran to the mail truck, jumped inside, only to find that when Dave turned the ignition, nothing happened.

"Bastards!" he yelled as he hit the steering wheel. "They sucked it dry!"

Darla sneered at him "And this is the society of assholes we're risking our lives for?"

Dave sighed and quickly thought of another plan. "Let's just take your car."

"We can't," she said, wincing. "Amy gave me a ride home. I left my car at work."

"Then I guess we're going to your work," he said.

"My work is too far away. It would take us forever to get there."

"Fine," he groaned. "We'll just take Mr. Pitman's car."

"All right." She reached for the door handle and opened the door.

She and Dave quickly jumped out of the mail truck. As Dave was walking around the other side, he heard Darla scream. He ran around just in time to prevent a walking dead man from making a meal out of her. Dave quickly slammed the axe into the side of the zombie's head and watched as the body fell to the ground. He retrieved the axe from its head, trying to ignore the bits of brain matter stuck to the blade.

"Darla," he said calmly. "I realize this is all a little much to take in, but you have to use the bat on these things before they kill you. Do you understand?"

She nodded her head nervously. Dave grabbed her hand and ran across the yard to Mr. Pitman's car. Then he stopped and went back to the corpse of his neighbor. After digging around in the body's pockets, he found the keys to the car.

"Get in the car," Dave said as Darla watched him.

She jumped in and he ran and climbed into the driver's side. He turned the ignition but with no luck. "Damn it!" he shouted.

"Well, I guess that explains why he never went anywhere," Darla said with a desperate sigh.

Just then thinking of Mr. Pitman, Dave realized he was forgetting something. "Where's Lilly?" he asked as he looked around nervously.

"I don't know," Darla said in a panic. "You had her last."

They had left her in the mail truck, and knowing there could be other zombies lurking around, they both leaped out of the car and dashed across the front lawn. They stopped in their tracks when they reached their driveway and saw three zombies circling the mail truck.

"Let's get them!" Dave shouted.

Together, they rushed the zombies. Blood and guts flew through the air as they hammered away at the skulls of the zombies threatening the life of their small pup. Dave got to the last one, who had figured out how to open the truck's door, and was looking at Lilly with hunger in its eyes.

Dave lunged forward and slammed the axe through the zombie's neck. The head fell to the pavement with a splat and the body buckled into a heap onto the ground. Dave quickly stepped over the body and saw Lilly sitting peacefully in her backpack. "Thank God!" he sighed. He quickly put the backpack on and reached for his cell phone.

"I don't think we can do this on our own," Darla said. "Three, four, even five we can handle, but you know there's more coming. Is there anyone you can call? Is there anyone crazy enough to have the same idea as we do?"

He thought about it for a second. "George!" he exclaimed as he flipped open his phone. "It's ringing!" he announced to Darla, as if she couldn't figure that out herself.

"George! It's Dave. Listen, can you come by and pick up me and my wife?"

There was a pause as Dave listened.

"We ran out of gas and we need a ride. We plan on taking these bastards out before they take over the whole city," Dave explained.

Darla watched as Dave got an angry look on his face. "Yes, I'm serious!" he said as if offended. "Look, just come by and pick us up." He paused for a second to wait for a response. "Okay, see you then," he responded, then slammed his phone shut angrily.

Darla looked at him intently.

"He's coming," Dave said.

"Good."

"Can you believe he laughed at me?" he said, shocked. "As if I'm not man enough to handle it."

Darla didn't say anything, she just smiled at him. He was covered in blood, holding a bloody axe, and carrying around a little white puffball of a dog in a backpack.

"No, honey," she said. "I can't imagine why he would do a thing like that."

They sat on the curb for ten minutes, and then heard loud music approaching. "Must be him," Dave said as he stood up.

Seconds later, a large green pickup truck came screeching around the bend at full speed. The truck came to a sudden stop right in front of them, and George, who was in the bed of the truck, motioned them aboard. "Come on up," he said happily, obviously strangely glad one of his conspiracy theories had come true.

Dave and Darla hopped in the rear bed of the pickup and George took off before they could even sit down. Both of them fell on their buts onto an arsenal of weapons.

"I see you weren't lying about the ammo and guns," Dave called as he looked around.

George smiled and glanced over his shoulder. "I see you brought your dog along."

"Yeah," Dave said, almost feeling embarrassed.

"That's cool," George grinned. "So did I." He then looked to the wide passenger seat where a dog and two other people were sitting. "This is Morris!"

Dave fell backwards as an enormous dog stuck its head through the small back window and started to growl ferociously.

"It's okay, boy," George said. Morris stuck his head back through the window and left the new arrivals alone.

"So, that was Morris," George began as he called back to them. "And this is my boy, Russ, and the man next to me is my bud Doyle. He doesn't say much."

George paused and looked at Dave and Darla in the rearview mirror. "I'm glad you called me, Dave. I really am. We have all these weapons, but we needed more hands to fire them. Can you both shoot?"

"Yes," Darla and Dave replied together.

"Really?" George asked in a surprised tone. "I wouldn't figure you to be a guy that was into that sort of thing."

"You didn't figure you'd ever see me looking like this, have you?" Dave asked.

George looked at Dave's blood-soaked clothes. "You got a point there," he said as he took a swig of beer. "So basically, this is what you have to do," George said. "We come across a group of zombies, we slow down and you open fire. You got it?"

"Yeah," Dave replied.

"Good," he said with an evil grin and dark chuckle. "Cause we're going to be circling the area around ground zero."

Dave and Darla just looked at each other in fear; that wasn't exactly what they had in mind when Dave called George for help.

"Well, that's probably where we'd find the most of them wandering around," Dave said, trying to hide his uncertainty.

They rode in silence until they pulled into a gas station.

Doyle got out and placed his gun in the belt of his pants. "We need a fill up, be on the lookout and watch my back," he said to Dave.

As they all sat watching Doyle to make sure no zombies were going to threaten him. They all jumped at the sound of Morris growling. Darla turned around to look at Dave and screamed when a zombie appeared right behind him.

Dave jumped to the other side of the truck and turned around to shoot the zombie right in the forehead with the gun George supplied him.

"Nice!" George shouted. "I'm impressed, Dave. I never saw someone react so fast."

George walked over to the other side of the truck and glanced down at the zombie lying on the ground. "You nearly emptied every bit of brains out of that one!" he said with a dark laugh.

"I'm glad you're pleased," Dave said, still trying to regain his composure.

Doyle had just finished filling up the pickup when dark clouds began to roll in. He hopped in the driver's seat and looked in his rearview mirror as he addressed his passengers. "We've got to hurry and get to ground zero before the rain comes in. There's no more risk of radiation, but I don't know how well you'll like getting rained on."

He revved the engine and peeled away from the desolate gas station, leaving no one but the one lone cashier that was holed up in the glass enclosed pit stop, looking nervously out the window.

With a full tank of gas, Doyle was ready for a fight. Dave just wondered why no one else was on the road, and why they were the only ones smart—or stupid enough—to think of fighting before the zombies got out of control. As they rode along, Dave could see there were apparently other groups of vigilantes out there with the same idea. He saw various zombies lying on the side of the road, some burning in piles, to prevent them from coming back.

Everything seemed quiet for the time being as Doyle sped down the highway to the graveyard. It seemed like most of the zombies had already been destroyed. As the approached the graveyard, a crack of lightning came down and struck a tree, and a spark of fire came shooting out from a telephone wire as the tree branch fell on top of it. The small spark gave way to a full on flame, sending smoke flying into the air.

Thunder rumbled as the clouds burst open and rain fell upon them like small, cold bullets. As the pickup made its way slowly up through the small, winding roads of the graveyard, the nightmare unfolded. Through their raindrop-soaked eyelids, Dave, George and Darla could see not fifty or a hundred undead roaming around, but more like two to three hundred.

"There's a sea of them!" Dave cried out through the pounding rain.

Doyle suddenly veered off the road and splashed through the muddy grass. He headed straight for the sea of undead and began taking them out one by one in his monstrous truck.

"Shoot them!" George cried out as they drove past the walking dead, the zombies reaching up with clawed hands and chasing after the truck. Dave and Darla started to shoot, taking most of the closest bodies out on the first try. Those that reached the truck and managed to run alongside, fell within seconds with bullets to the head.

"Get back on the paved road!" George told Doyle. The mud was slowing them down and the walking dead seemed to have turned into much faster creatures, nearly climbing into the rear bed of the pickup as the vehicle slowly drove through the storm-darkened cemetery. The zombies nearest to them all fell to the ground from a bullet to the brain, but there were others in the distance, coming their way.

Suddenly, the truck got stuck in the mud. Zombies were getting closer as the wide tires spun unproductively, spraying wet earth behind it. One zombie in the way was covered from head to tow and it fell over, blinded, dirt clogging its mouth.

"Stop accelerating!" George yelled. "You're just digging us in deeper!"

George looked out into the open field of graves; he could see figures moving in on them, stumbling and crawling.

"Come on, Dave, help me out," George yelled as he hopped down off the truck.

"What are you doing?" Darla shouted after Dave, when he too, jumped down. "Don't worry; we're going to get us out of here. Just shoot them, Darla. Don't let them get close."

As Dave and George pushed the back of the truck to try and lift it out of the mud, Doyle pressed on the accelerator. Darla was shooting, and took out a good twenty of the walking dead who were getting close. As the tires whirred in the mud, the zombies began to pick up speed, closing in on them. Darla squeezed the trigger but the gun was empty, and she didn't have time to reach for another clip, seeing another zombie approaching Dave and George from behind.

Acting fast, she grabbed the axe lying next to her and buried it in the zombie's skull, leaving it stuck there just as the truck broke free and Dave and George ran behind, to then hop into the back.

Once safe inside the truck bed, Doyle drove faster.

"Now get back on the damn pavement!" George shouted to Doyle, who did as he was told.

Doyle slowed down and drove through the darkness of the tree-lined, paved roads of the graveyard. The cemetery that was once a haven where the dead rested was now the playground for them to run around, eating the flesh of the living.

The vigilantes in the truck, as they began to call themselves, were not about to let them take over the world. The living had above ground, and the dead had below it.

They wanted to send a message to the walking dead, that even though they were once loved, they were no longer welcome on the Earth. The once peaceful cemetery had become a war zone. The silence of the graveyard, once filled with the soft murmurs of a priest's prayers to the newly deceased, was now filled with the moans of the undead as they chased down the living to clean their bones.

The sound of gunfire echoed amongst the tombstones, as the living stopped the undead from walking the Earth forever.

POST OFFICE OF THE DEAD

ANTHONY GIANGREGORIO

"Come on, people, listen up, there's a lot to cover and there's not much time," Fred, the supervisor for Branch 32, yelled out. He was standing at a podium in a small, stuffy room, and before him, in twenty metal chairs, were the mail carriers for the north section of the city.

Everyone was talking, their voices rising and falling in pitch as each person tried to share their stories of the night before.

It had been a hell of a yesterday, too.

For some unknown reason, the recently deceased had returned to life and were now feasting on the living.

So far the outbreak, or whatever it was, had been contained, the United States now under martial law. It had been found out early that a bite would infect someone and cause them to become one of the walking dead.

People were told to remain in their homes, barricading themselves in until the crisis passed, but despite this, despite the dead walking, the mail still needed to get through.

There were already bins of mail and packages piled in the back room, and if the post office stopped for even one week, they would become so buried in mail they would never recover, so today, though the dead were walking, so too would the postal carriers of Branch 32.

"This is crazy, Fred," Jodi called out from the side of the room. Next to her was Chris, a tall man who topped six feet. The two had been friends for years and he looked out for Jodi like a big brother.

Fred sighed from the podium as he glared back at Jodi. He saw a pretty woman in her late thirties with piercing blue eyes and dark black hair. One time, years ago he had broken protocol and had had an affair with her, but he'd ended it before his wife could find out. Jodi hadn't taken it too well, but now, years later, the two were friends again.

"Crazy? Why? We deliver in any other disaster, don't we? Thunderstorms, blizzards, wildfires, hell, we deliver in floods if the houses are still intact. The mail must go through, that's our motto, right?"

Jodi crossed her arms over her chest and frowned, Chris doing the same in the seat beside her.

"That's horseshit, Fred, there's nothin' in the manual about the mail must get delivered when the dead walk," Chris said.

"Why?" Fred defended himself. "What's the difference? It's a natural disaster, that's all. We deliver in gang neighborhoods and we deliver where murders have taken place. This is just one more obstacle to overcome."

A man with a large belly and thin legs stood up and pointed at Fred accusingly. "Then why don't you go out there and deliver the damn mail yourself!" he shouted.

Fred grinned. "Why? 'Cause I'm the supervisor. I get paid to supervise you knuckleheads and that's what I'm gonna do."

"This is nuts," Jodi said, a few others agreeing.

Fred slammed the palm of his hand on the wooden podium. "Enough, quiet down, dammit!"

The crowd settled and all eyes went to Fred. A few low murmurs were still filtering from the crowd, but Fred knew this was as good as it gets.

"Okay, so today is no different from any other day you deliver," he began. The murmur grew louder and Fred raised his voice, repeating himself. "I said, this is no different than any other day. You just need to be careful out there, that's all. And to make sure you stay safe, the higher-ups have agreed to give you some more gear to protect yourselves out there other than your key-chain mace."

"Like what?" Chris asked, his curiosity peaked.

Fred pulled a two-way radio from his belt and talked into it. "Bring the stuff in, George."

All eyes turned to the one door in the room when it opened and another, lower class supervisor came in holding a large box. There were four more managers behind George.

Chris chuckled as the men walked in and set down their burdens. "Christ, when you put all the damn managers and supervisors in one place there's like one for every five of us carriers, it's crazy."

Fred frowned when he heard Chris' comment but others were talking now, the sound level going up in pitch.

"Okay, okay, quiet down so I can pass these out," Fred said as he went to George, who nodded a hello.

The other managers began taking items from the box and passing them out to each of the carriers. When Jodi received hers, her eyes went wide as she held a weapon in each hand.

"You have got to be kidding me. A gun and a machete? To deliver mail?"

"Yes, that's exactly what you need to deliver the mail. And there will be one more thing added to the list. You will all be issued plastic armor, similar to what hockey players wear. It's lightweight and is more than enough to stop a bite if one of the dead get too close."

Chris shook his head as he studied the gun in his hand. It was small, .22 pistol. "This is unbelievable. It's like a fucking horror movie."

Fred heard Chris' comment and replied, "Maybe so, but these weapons and the armor will keep you safe and that's all that matters." He walked closer to the crowd as they talked amongst themselves. "Look, people, it's a whole new world out there. No one knows how long the dead will walk. For all we know, this could go on forever. But if so, then we still have a job to do. So stay sharp, watch out for blind spots, and make sure you wear your armor." He clapped his hands loudly. "Okay, get going and be safe out there."

While a few stayed in their seats, most stood up, gathered their new equipment and headed out to gather their mail, load the vans and postal vehicles and deliver their routes.

They knew Fred was correct. Though the dead walked, they were mail carriers. They delivered in any weather, in any disaster; they were the heartbeat of a nation.

The mail had to go through, and even zombies couldn't stop it.

Jodi pulled up in her white LLV Government Issue vehicle and parked in front of a large Victorian mansion. All the homes on the street were the same size… too big. One name Jodi used for the oversized houses was McMansion, meaning far too enormous for one single family to live in.

It was the rich part of town and Jodi had been on this particular route for over three years. She knew everyone and they knew her. At Christmas time, more than half of her customers left her a Christmas tip and the extra money was a welcome extra to her salary.

There were even a few customers who would chat with her, most being senior citizens. They would wait for her each day during the hot summer months with a can of soda or a bottle of cold water.

Many had become defacto friends and she always had time to pet a dog or a cat sitting on a porch or in a front yard. She liked her job and did it well, and planned on doing it until she retired.

One more thing Jodi always did, as did other postal carriers, was to keep their eyes and ears open for trouble. Many lives had been saved by a postal carrier who had peered into a window after seeing the mail piling up on the porch or in the mailbox. There were people who had no family, and the only ones to visit them, though only technically, were the carriers leaving the mail.

So the postal carrier was the watchdog of the neighborhood, always on the lookout for trouble.

Opening the rear door to her postal vehicle, Jodi reached inside and took out the large package for the McMansion she was parked in front of. It had been too big to carry, so she planned on delivering it first, then she would drive to the next spot where she would park and continue her route.

From the street, she had to walk a good thirty feet to the front door of the home, as were most of the houses on the street. They were all set far back with large, manicured front lawns, water displays and expensive flowers.

Shifting her plastic armor to make it fit better, and making sure her new weapons were secure, Jodi picked up the package and began walking up the granite walkway. She felt ridiculous with the gear on, but she also knew it was necessary.

As she approached the front door, she paused halfway there to see it was open. Looking left and right, there was no one else on the street. It was early morning and well after morning rush hour; children were in school and now was the time for mothers and others to relax before the day truly began.

When she was ten feet from the ajar front door, she studied the opening, figuring the owner of the house had seen her pull up and had come to the door in anticipation, so she didn't give it much thought.

But as she reached the steps and began to ascend them, she stopped in her tracks when she heard a low moan, like someone was hurt.

She didn't feel threatened, assuming someone needed help. But as she reached the doorway and was about to call out, a shape popped up and blocked the entryway.

Jodi's mouth fell open at the sight greeting her. She had never seen a real zombie before, but had only heard about them from others as well as what she saw on TV. But the reality of it was far more visceral than she would have ever believed.

Before her, swaying back and forth, was the owner of the house. The old woman was in her seventies, with white hair and wrinkled and sagging skin that made her look like she had put on a dress suit that was two sizes too big.

She was naked, her hair soaked with water as well as blood.

If Jodi had to guess what had happened, she assumed the old woman had fallen in the tub while bathing, had cracked her head on the tub, which had killed her, and then had revived as one of the walking dead.

"Mrs. Carlson, it's me, Jodi," she said, not knowing what else to do. "I have a package for you, but you need to sign for it."

The old woman merely moaned louder and took a step towards her. Jodi, realizing quickly she was in danger, threw the package at the old woman, turned and ran, saying over her shoulder, "Forget it, you don't need to sign for it."

Behind her, Mrs. Carlson stumbled onto the porch and down the stairs. She wasn't very coordinated and she slipped on the third stair. She tumbled face first onto the granite of the walkway, smashing her nose and cracking her forehead. Teeth snapped from the blunt force trauma, and as the old woman tried to pick herself up, she spit bloody globules of saliva and teeth.

Jodi barely saw any of this. She ran to her postal vehicle, unlocked it, climbed in and drove off with a screech of tires.

The only thing she kept remembering was that back when she took the test to apply for the letter carrier's position, there had never been anything on it about zombies.

Jodi pulled in to the local donut shop ten minutes later, deciding it was time for a break. As she drove to the shop, she had seen six zombies stumbling about the road, like drunkards late for a frat party. She had ignored them and focused on the road ahead.

Getting out of the postal truck, she walked to the entrance and stepped inside the shop. She was relieved to see Chris and Jim were there already, with steaming cups of coffee and a donut before each of them.

Chris saw her enter and waved her to join them.

"Hi, Jodi, how's your morning going?" Chris asked with a smile.

She quickly filled him in on her adventure with Mrs. Carlson and both Chris and Jim shook their heads at the end of her story.

"Wow, at least you got out of there in one piece," Chris said. "I found the mother of a family on First Street eating her two kids. They were three and four years old. I called the police and they said they'd get someone over there as fast as they could, but as you can imagine, they're pretty busy."

"How come you didn't just shoot her with the gun you got?" Jodi asked as she sipped her coffee after the waitress came over and poured her a cup. It was a down home donut shop—not a franchise—where a waitress took your order and topped off you coffee. The three postal carriers had been going there for years.

"Why?" Chris asked. "Because if I did, there would be all kinds of paperwork to fill out. At least that's what Fred told me before I left today. Trust me on this one, Jodi, don't kill any zombies unless you have no choice. Let the cops handle it."

"Amen to that," Jim said as he took a bite of his donut.

There was a commotion outside and all three of them looked up and out the plate glass window to see that five zombies had wandered into the parking lot from the street. Two were men and the other three were women, the ages ranging from twenty to thirty. All five had gaping wounds in their necks and torso and each of them had died painfully from vicious attacks.

As the three postal workers watched through the window, their new realty hit home just a little more. People coming and going from the donut shop ran from the five zombies, more than one screaming for help.

That help arrived seconds later when two squad cars and a SWAT van rolled up and disgorged Kevlar wearing men. They formed a perimeter around the five zombies, and before any of the walking dead could so much as moan, they were shot down in a barrage of lead that blew arms off bodies and took three of their heads off in a glorious spray of blood and brain matter. A pink mist hung in the air, all that was left of the destroyed heads.

As each of the ghouls was taken down, men with body bags began stuffing each corpse into them. In minutes, the five bodies were encased in the black bags and unceremoniously tossed into the back of the SWAT van.

The two squad cars waved onlookers away, climbed back into the vehicles, then drove off, a few blips of the siren as they reentered traffic.

The SWAT van pulled out and was soon gone, and the only thing left of the scene of carnage was the pools of dark blood still spread on the pavement in the parking lot.

As the three postal employees watched the now empty scene, one of the donut shop employees appeared while dragging a garden hose. Calmly, like he was washing spilled red paint, he began spraying the blood and diluting it, until there was nothing left but a few faded spots that would also disappear when it dried.

"Well, that was interesting," Chris said as he looked at the others.

"Shit, did you see how fast the cops arrived? And now it's like nothing ever happened," Jim said.

"What do you think it all means?" Jodi asked.

Chris shrugged his broad shoulders. "If I had to guess, I'd say the cops or the establishment or whoever's running the show is trying to act like this whole dead walking thing is nothing but an inconvenience."

Jim leaned forward. "You mean like a conspiracy?"

"No, stupid," Chris joked. "I mean they don't want to admit we have a serious problem on our hands here. There trying to keep it all quiet. You know, like when a zombie pops up. They get in there, take it down, then take off, leaving things exactly like it was before."

"That's crazy," Jodi said. "Surely they realize this is serious."

Chris looked her in the face. "Oh come on, Jodi, How many times have our leaders tried to sweep something under the rug, even if it's dire to the point of being global?"

"He's got a point there," Jim added as he finished his donut.

Jodi checked her wristwatch. "Well, whatever's happening, there's nothing we can do about it now. Breaks over, I've got to get back to work." She stood up.

Chris checked his watch and nodded as well, then Jim did the same. "Shit, you're right, I gotta go too." He stood up. "Okay, you guys be careful out there."

"Same to you, Chris," Jim said and Jodi added her own well wishes.

The three carriers left the donut shot with a wave to the clerk, climbed into their postal vehicles and headed off in different directions to finish their routes.

Jodi had been delivering for about three hours when she came upon a letter that needed a signature confirmation.

Walking up to the front door, she rang the doorbell and waited. As she waited, she shifted uncomfortably in her protective gear. It was hot out and the gear only made her hotter. She desperately wanted to take it off, but knew it would be tantamount to suicide.

She had already decided tomorrow she was going to call in sick and reevaluate her future. Maybe she'd transfer to being a clerk.

No one had answered the door and she was about to ring it again when she heard a loud thump come from the other side of the door.

"Hello? Is anyone there?" she called. "I need a signature on a letter, please."

A low moan came to her ears but with the ambient noise such as the traffic on the street, it sounded more like, *"Leeeavvve iiitttt."*

"I'm sorry, I can't leave it. You need to sign for it." She waited for a reply and when none came, said, "Hello, did you hear me?"

There was no answer and ten second later there was another thump.

Reaching for the doorknob, she found the door locked. There was a mail slot on the door and she knelt down and pushed it open with her fingers. Peering into the house, she saw the reason why the home owner wasn't answering the door.

He was dead.

In his late eighties at least, the man looked like he'd had a heart attack or some such malady that had definitely killed him. His skin was pale and his eyes sunken and one leg didn't seem to work too well. If Jodi assumed correctly, the man might have been dead for a few days before he had risen as one of the undead.

"Great, he's dead, what the hell am I supposed to do now?" she said to no one.

The old man stumbled around the foyer, bumping into walls and a small end table.

Jodi watched him for more than a minute and decided there was nothing she could do.

"Oh, the hell with it," she mumbled as she took out a pen, scribbled the man's name on the line where the signature was supposed to be, then slid the letter into the slot. "If they don't like it they can fire me," she muttered as she stepped back and returned to her vehicle.

A half hour later she had another package to delivery that required yet another signature. Normally, her day was filled with delivery and signature confirmations, but now, with the dead walking, they seemed to have taken on an entirely new meaning.

The house before her was a single story ranch house with a manicured lawn and yellow flowers lining the walkway.

At least, that's how she remembered it.

Now, it looked like something out of a war movie.

A ten foot, electrified chain-link fence lined the property and sandbags were scattered and piled waist high across the lawn. To the right, where there used to be a birdbath, there was now a four foot fox hole, complete with machine gun emplacement.

Jodi slowly waked up to the chained gate and tried to take in the fort before her.

There was an intercom tied to the gate with wire and she pressed the button, not knowing what else to do.

A crackled static filled the intercom and then a male voice, said, "Go away!"

She blinked in surprise at the rudeness, turned to look around the street, glad to see it was devoid of the living or undead, and pressed the button again.

More static filled the intercom and a gruff voice replied, "Fuck off, I don't want any."

She pressed the button once more and received a similar epitaph.

"Uhm, hello in there, it's the mail carrier. I need a signature for a package," she said quickly.

"Just leave it," the reply came quick and curt.

"Uhm, I can't. I need a signature. Look, if you don't come out I'll bring it back and you can go to the post office and pick it up there."

There was silence for a few seconds and then, "I can't do that. Till the zombies stop walking, I won't leave my house. It's the friggin' apocalypse, didn't you know that? Just leave it at the gate. I'll get it after you leave."

"I'm sorry, but I can't do that. Until it's signed for it's my responsibility. So either come out or I'm leaving."

"How do I know you're not one of them?"

"What? A zombie?" she asked incredulously.

"Yeah, one of *them*."

"Ah, well, 'cause I can talk? I don't think they can talk, at least I haven't met one that could. Have you?"

"No, not yet. They're stupid. Hell, they're dead."

"That's what I heard," she said, sounding bored.

"I heard it's from a satellite in space that's in Earth's orbit. It's giving off radiation. Either way, I'm not coming out."

"Fine, then I'm going. I'll leave the pink ticket here on the ground. It has the number of your item. So long," she said and turned to leave.

"No wait, don't go. Fine, I'll come out. I need that package. It's water purification tablets for when the water stops flowing in the tap."

"So you're coming out?"

"Yes, just give me a second to get dressed."

She sighed. "Fine, but please don't take too long. I have a schedule to keep and I'm running late as it is." She scratched her arm, the weight of the plastic armor uncomfortable, and the machete on her hip was heavy.

She waited for over five minutes and was about to leave when the front door of the home opened and a man wearing a gas mask and body armor stepped out.

As he walked down the pathway, she saw he carried a double barrel shotgun.

When he reached her, he opened the gate after looking around the street and said, "You know, miss, you really should be somewhere safe, not walking around on the street."

"Thank you for your concern. Here, sign this, please," she said as she handed the man a clipboard and pen. The brown, paper-wrapped package was on the ground at her feet. He quickly signed and handed her back the clip board. He was about to bend over and take the package when he suddenly went rigid. Jodi realized he was looking over her shoulder and she turned around to see a zombie heading right for her.

It was a middle-aged male with a large wound on the right side of its neck. The zombie had been attacked and killed and once died, had returned.

"Stand back, miss, I got this," the man said as he leveled the shotgun at the ghoul. Before Jodi could say anything, she was pushed behind the man and her ears were ringing as the man gave the zombie both barrels.

The first barrage of buckshot tore the ghoul's right arm off, and the second took the head off like it was made of wet newspaper. Blood geysered up and out of the stump as the body toppled over, the remaining arm flailing on the ground as the feet kicked up and down like a child having a tantrum. The man admired his marksmanship with a wan smile.

"Look at 'im spurt. Never understood why that is."

"What do you mean?" Jodi asked as she waited for the ringing in her ears to fade. She looked away from the headless corpse, not wanting to look at all the blood.

"The blood, miss, the blood. I never understood how those damn things can bleed if they're dead. After all, their hearts don't work any more, right? So if that's so, then why do they bleed when you shoot 'em?"

Jodi could have cared less and she told the man so. With a nod, she left him and went back to her postal vehicle, locking the doors when she was inside it.

No sooner did she do this then a pale face slapped her window. It was a woman, or had been once. Now it was a withered shell that looked like it had crawled out of the grave. Maggots squirmed about in the nose and ear canals and the eyes were bleach white orbs of nothingness. As Jodi stared at the face, the zombie slid its cheek against the glass, leaving a smudge of puss and other fluids thanks to decomposition. A few maggots stuck to the glass, wiggling free to fall to the warm pavement where they would soon die.

Jodi, trying to remain calm, knowing she was safe inside the vehicle, slid the ignition key into the ignition, turned it, and slowly began to drive.

The ghoul walked with her for a few feet and then began to fall away.

As she put some distance between herself and the zombie, she glanced in her side mirror. As she did, a boom echoed across the street and the zombie went down minus a head, decapitated at the neck. She leaned forward so she could see the far side of the street and the man in the gas mask was walking over to the zombie, admiring his latest kill. She watched as he shot the ghoul's severed head, blowing it into a hundred pieces, a pink mist floating in the air before the wind dispersed it.

Then she turned the corner and the scene was lost from sight. She was glad it was.

Jodi parked her postal vehicle in the parking lot of Branch 32 and went inside. She was tired. It had been a long day.

Going to her locker, she took off her gear, placed the gun and machete in her locker—glad she hadn't had to use either one—and changed into her street clothes.

On her way out of the building, she spotted Chris and Jim near their cars, talking together. Chris was louder than usual, waving his arms in the air as he discussed something that he was emotional about.

"Hi, guys, what's going on?" Jodi asked as she got within earshot of the two men.

Chris turned at the sound of her voice and smiled. He was always glad to see her.

"Jodi, good, now I'll get someone on my side of this discussion."

"What are you talking about?" She nodded hello to Jim who gave her a nod of his own.

"You won't believe what management is going to try to do by the end of the week," Chris said, and when Jodi didn't say anything, he continued. "They're gonna start using zombies as extra help."

"What? That's crazy. Why?" she asked.

"Because we're short handed, that's why. Between all the PTFs leaving and all the people that have quit this week, there's not enough manpower to deliver all the mail," Chris said.

"But how can a zombie deliver mail?" she asked.

Jim spoke up. "That's just the thing, Jodi, they won't be delivering the real mail, so to speak. Just the circulars and flyers and junk mail, like those post cards the politicians have us deliver during voting season."

"They didn't waste any time," Chris said angrily. "Hasn't been two weeks and the guys upstairs are figuring out how to make a buck on this dead walking thing."

"Chris is upset about it," Jim told Jodi.

"Damn straight I am. They think a zombie can do our job, is that it?" he demanded.

Jim shook his head. "No, Chris, of course not, don't get upset. It makes sense though. Those circulars only have 'resident' on them. Anyone with half a brain can deliver them. It's all the rest that needs a competent person to make sure they get to the right address, forwards, stopped mail, ect."

"But what about our jobs, Jim? Next thing you know, they'll have zombies doing our jobs, too." He shook his right index finger as his face grew redder by the second. "I'll tell you both right now, I'm not sitting still for this. Tomorrow, first thing in the morning, I'll be talking to our union rep. I'll get to the bottom of this." He waved curtly, turned and head for his car. "I'll see you guys tomorrow. I'm going home to see what I can get started on. This isn't right, they can't do this and damn it I'm gonna stop it. The post office is my life. I'll die before I let them dead bastards take my job." He climbed into his car and drove off with a quick beep of his horn and screeching tires.

Jodi looked at Jim who returned her gaze.

"Looks like he's at it again," she said.

Jim nodded. "Yeah, he's like a dog with a bone, too. Were never gonna hear the end of this till it's over."

"I'm not looking forward to the next week with him, I'll tell you that right now," she said.

"Ditto for me. All we can do is nod when he talks and hope he blows himself out eventually."

She paused before speaking. "Do you really think they'll get zombies to pick up the slack for us?"

He shrugged. "Anything's possible. Shit, after some of the idiots I've worked with, maybe the zombies will be smarter. Remember that woman who was stealing cell phones? Or the guy who was dumping his undelivered mail in a storage locker every night?"

"Yeah, you do have a point there. We've had some real winners get hired, haven't we."

"Damn straight," he said. He checked his watch. "I gotta go. Susan's making veal parm tonight and I told her I wouldn't be later than six."

"Okay, have a good night," she said.

They both went to their vehicles and drove off, another day done.

Jodi drove around a few zombies in the streets but made it home without difficulty. Once inside, she locked the doors and windows and settled down for a quiet night at home.

Tomorrow would be another day.

"Where's Chris?" she asked at the morning gathering.

Jim shook his head. "No one knows. He didn't call in sick and there's no answer at his house. And his cars not in his driveway."

"Oh God, you don't think…" she began, not wanting to voice her fears.

"That the dead got him on his way home last night?" Jim suggested. "Could be, we'll just have to wait and see if he turned up."

Jodi nodded, knowing Jim was right. People were disappearing every day it seemed and she prayed Chris was all right. But until then, she needed to focus on her job and staying alive.

The next two weeks went by quickly for Jodi. The dead were still walking and things were slowly growing worse. The Government was still doing its best to contain the walking dead, but each day it seemed the situation was growing worse.

Jodi was pulling into the parking lot one morning when she saw there was a commotion in the back lot.

After parking her car, she went to see what was going on. She found Jim and ten other postal workers watching two large trucks pulling into the lot. But where normally the trucks would be carrying bins of mail, there was something inside them that had never been transported before.

As the rear doors were rolled up, men wearing heavy armor and carrying cattle prods began herding zombies out of the two trucks. Jodi watched in awe as the ghouls were made to line up. Each wore a blue postal shirt and the blue baseball caps all employees were mandated to wear.

Jim moved up next to her and she turned to look at him. "What's going on, Jim? What are they doing here?"

He sighed. "I was talking to one of the managers before you arrived. You remember a few weeks ago, back when Chris disappeared and how he was telling us about some program to get the dead to deliver circulars and junk mail?"

She nodded.

"Well, here they are, all trained and ready to go."

"But it's crazy. They can't deliver mail; they're dead for Christ's sake."

"That they are."

"Do they get paid?" she asked as she studied the pale, slack faces.

"Yeah, but trust me, you don't want to know with what."

As she watched the ghouls herded to the rear of the building by the trainers, her mouth fell open when she spotted Chris in the back of the line. His face was pale, flies buzzing around his head, and there was an eye missing as well as an ear. He had a chunk of his throat torn out, but with his shirt collar pulled high it was hard to see.

"Oh my God, that's Chris over there. Jim, look, Chris is one of them," she gasped quickly. "Chris, Chris!" she yelled to him. "It's me, Jodi. Chris!"

"I don't think he can hear you anymore, Jodi," Jim said sadly. "I guess we know where he went. He must have been attacked and ended up as one of them. Poor guy, I'm gonna miss him." He turned to walk away. "I'm going inside; it's almost time to punch in." He was shaking his head as he walked away.

Jodi wouldn't leave, not yet. As Chris came within a few feet of her, only the trainers keeping him in line, she called out to him again.

Chris slowed and then stopped, holding up the zombies behind him and he turned to face Jodi, as if he recognized her face and her voice. But then he continued on, brain dead and stupid.

"At least he's still doing his job," she said to no one. "He said he'd die before he let them make him quit."

With nothing to do to help him, she went to punch in, starting a new day in a dead world.

But there was one difference this day. Now she knew Chris was gone for good. The mystery of his disappearance had been solved.

She was really going to miss him.

Z DAY

AARON ALPER

A loud noise jars me awake. I still feel tired. Damn Ambien. What was that anyway? A bomb or something? A bomb? Oh no. My body stiffens with fear.

I dash from the bed, to the window of my shitty little garage apartment, and gaze over the backyards of the houses that line my Old Northeast neighborhood.

I can immediately see the source of the damage. Smoke and flames mostly. I don't think it was a bomb. The smoke clears for a second and I can make out something through it. A plane! Oh my God. A plane has crashed in my neighbor's yard! I wish I knew his name. That ugly fellow who always tends his garden, which never seems to look nice.

I can hear screaming in the distance. Not too much fire, which is kind of surprising, but a lot of smoke, and it's engulfing the bougainvillea. The screaming continues. Wow. Whoever is doing that has quite a set of pipes.

What brought the plane down? Was it terrorists? No. Terrorists in St. Petersburg seems unlikely. I look to the streets, which were already starting to show signs of panic. My neighbors are outside. Even the ugly fellow. Wow. He really is quite ugly.

Something roars overhead. A helicopter. Now I am curious.

Still in my night clothes, I run downstairs to the street and approach the group of loud neighbors. I don't want to ask them what happened, mainly because I find them odd and really hate their dogs, those barky little schnauzers who I just want to shake. The neighbors huddle, loud voices and questions. No one knows what happened. I stare at the plane, which is much cooler up close. The tale end is now on fire, but the cockpit seems okay. They call that a cockpit, right?

Through the cracked window someone is moving. They're alive! Perhaps maybe I should help them.

Suddenly, the door of the cockpit swings open, and a man crawls out, screaming in what sounds like terrible pain. He struggles for a moment, screams once, then collapses as if fainting. No, not fainting…dead.

There's movement behind him. A passenger, a blonde-haired woman. Bourgeoisie Elitist type hair-do. They probably own three planes. Lucky them. Though not so lucky now, I suppose. The woman is now climbing over the man. She looks as though she's checking his pulse. No, wait. She isn't. She's grabbing his head and pulling it back. She ripped it off!

Everyone watching screams in unison as blood sprays from the man's gaping neck.

I decide it's time to go inside now.

I run back to my apartment and slam the door. What did I just see? I quickly run to the television and snap it on, clicking frantically until I find Bay News 9. The anchorwoman, Erica Riggins, who is really quite lovely most of the time, appears on the screen, frantic even under her professionally veneer gloss.

"As we've just reported, a two-seater plane has crashed in the Old Northeast neighborhood of St. Petersburg. Reports are speculative as to what caused the crash and we're currently unaware as to whether the incident is connected with the recent rash of reports of the dead coming back to life and attacking the living."

My jaw drops open.

Erica Riggins continues. "As strange as it sounds, it has been confirmed that the dead, which city officials are declaring to be called zombies…" She pauses. She looks a bit lost. "…Are in fact returning to life and attacking the living. This situation has reached a pandemic within the past sixteen hours, and has caused waves of panic and destruction over the Bay area, as well as all over most cities over the state of Florida."

Erica Riggins checks the papers in front of her. "Reports from Washington account that this is indeed a nationwide, and worldwide phenomena. Accounts of zombies have even been reported in places as far as London, Germany, India and Japan."

I continue to stare at the TV.

"275 and Gandy Boulevard, as reported from the Bay News 9 helicopter, are completely clogged and reports of accidents and causalities are incalculable. All police and firemen have been dispatched to their respective areas, but authorities are still pensive about what the public's best course of action is. They're advised to stay in their places of residence until further information is released."

"For those of you just tuning in, I repeat. The dead are coming back to life and are attacking the living."

Erica Riggins voice echoes in my head.

The dead are coming back to life and are attacking the living.

Suddenly I snap back to reality.

Fucking A.

Finally!

A wave of excitement washes over me. Could it be? Is Z-Day here! After all these years of hoping and praying? Has it finally come? Could it be true? I better check. I peek out the window to look at the plane. The neighbors have fled and the woman who ate her husband was already teetering through the front yard, her face covered in blood.

Yes! It would appear that God, in His infinite wisdom, had taken heed of my request, and has rendered up a Zombie Apocalypse.

The time for action is upon me. I need to dress. I run from the window to my closet, swing open the door, and begin rummaging through my clothes. Oh, it's rather messy here, not much room at all. I pause. What the hell could I wear during a Zombie Apocalypse?

Flannel?

No wait. Flannel in Florida? Would that be all right? I'd probably be too hot. No, it's okay. I would be heading north anyway. The ground freezes during the winter up north. Which will keep the zombies down. Besides, everyone worth their weight in horror movie salt knows that flannel is an excellent print to wear when faced with hordes of the undead. People look good in it. It conjures up a rustic Pennsylvania feel…Monroeville.

Wait, what was I doing? Oh yes, flannel. And blue jeans. Dark blue jeans. They'll go better with the flannel. Too bad they're not bellbottoms. Those would have gone really good with the flannel. Talk about the classic *Dawn of the Dead* look. Why the hell don't they make bellbottoms anymore?

No time to think about that now. They're probably is less of a chance of bellbottoms being made now that zombies have arrived. I put on my jeans and my flannel, and run to put on some boots. Flip-flops would be nice in the Florida heat, but running from zombies in flip-flops ? Absolutely ridiculous.

Better see if there are any of them outside. I peek out the window to the site of the carnage. My neighbor's yard appears empty, except for the burning plane with the headless man in it. The plane woman zombie has moved on. No visible dead in front. Now to check the back.

I run from my living room to my bedroom.

Good, no zombies in the alleyway.

No, wait! I see some. At least I think they're zombies. Maybe they're homeless people. You can't really tell the difference. They're both shambling and slow.

The TV continues to play in the background.

"We have some eyewitness reports that almost all freeways and roads are undriveable. We repeat; if you are in a car, try your best to stay away from main roads."

I scoff at Erica. Who would be stupid enough to take their car during a Zombie Apocalypse? Don't these fools know anything? You go by foot.

"We have just received a video report from a witness of some of these dead attacks. We now go to the video."

A woman appears on the screen. She looks like my boss, with nice clothes, but has a face that could crack a mirror.

What the hell am I doing? I need weapons. I dash back to the messy closet, and grab my machete, and guns which I purchased specifically for this occasion, after reading a survival guide about zombies. I only got halfway through it. I probably should have read it all the way through, but it was so redundant. My mistake.

I find the machete right away, but the guns take a second. Where the hell is it? It's in that Steve Madden shoe box. Aha! Found it. I pull the gun out from the box, along with the strap I purchased, and hook it on myself. Lovely weapon. Wish I knew how to fire it. I suppose I should have taken lessons down at the gun shop. But I'm sure it will work in a pinch.

I run back into the living room to listen to Erica Riggins, but not before I catch a glimpse of myself in the mirror, in full flannel, machete, gun-strap glory.

Handsome zombie killer!

The TV continues. "There has been no official statement made by the White House whether or not military action will be taken. It appears that no further reasons have been released as to why the dead are coming back to life and devouring human flesh."

The answer is obvious. It's either gas from Venus or a rabid monkey.

Now I need food. I make way to the kitchen, and empty out the contents of my backpack, everything falling out everywhere with a loud crash. All of my school papers and my brand new copy of *The Picture of Dorian Gray*. It looks like I bent the cover. Damn. Oh well. I want to bring it, but I need room in my bag for food, and leisure reading during the apocalypse seems unlikely.

I fling open my pantry doors, perhaps a little too dramatically, because I unhinge them and send them crashing to the floor. I glance in the pantry. Tabbed cans of tuna fish. Cashews. Peanut butter. All of these will do nicely. High calorie, high protein, no sugar. Good energy. I bet I can live in a zombie world and still be on Atkins. That would be great. I'll be in magnificent shape. I pile the items in my bag, and then run to the window to check on my zombie friends. Out back is all right but I see that there are definitely more possible homeless zombies-types. They're too far away to see clearly. And they're slow, thank God! A Zombie Apocalypse with fast zombies is cool, but it seems unfair. How is anybody supposed to get anything done? They run at you like cheetahs, and they roar. But these zombies are slow and they haven't made any cheetah moves so far and they don't roar. I can hear them and they moan, though. It's kind of creepy, but then again, that's all part of the fun!

The zombies shamble down the street and one is close enough for me to look at its face. It is a nasty bluish-white, and it has milky eyes, and fresh dried blood surrounding what's left of yellow, chomping teeth. I'll be damned! It is that homeless man after all. Oh, the irony! I watch his teeth gnash on empty air as he stumbles down the street, lurching his way closer to the stairs. I think he can smell me. Suddenly, I have a realization.

I forgot to lock my door.

I better do it now.

Stomping like a rhino, I run to the kitchen and lock the door. Is there anything else I forgot? The windows are fine, they're too high off the ground for a zombie to reach. Or are they? Perhaps these zombies can climb? I don't think I have anyway of knowing. Time will tell, I guess.

I shake myself back to reality. I have my machete, guns, food, phone, and flannel. Do I need my wallet? Probably not, but better safe than sorry.

It's time to leave now. Oh, I feel all a twitter, like it is graduation day. I brace myself. The time has come where you can tell the quick from the dead. And I can do an eight minute mile.

I snap my backpack on and walk to the front door. The zombies will no doubt be waiting for me outside. Good! They're gonna meet the business end of my machete! I am the lion and they are the gazelle. Wait. That's a poor analogy, considering they're the ones that want to eat me. Then I'm the hunter and they're the gazelle. That's better.

I take a deep breath and open the door.

I'm immediately greeted by several living dead. They're much more disgusting up close, and the smell is astonishing. A couple of them—a woman in a business suit, and a man wearing an Abercrombie tank top—come at me. Their arms are outstretched, eyes empty, teeth gnashing. Acting fast, and squealing with glee, I swing the machete around full force like a baseball bat, knocking the zombies over the railing of my apartment stairs. I wait until I hear them rustle into the bushes of the house below, then peek over the edge. They both were on the ground, thrashing around, the way turtles do when put on their backs. It didn't kill them but they were out of the way. Their necks are gushing gore and blood everywhere—nice.

I bounce down the stairs, gracefully, careful not to slice myself with the machete, and jump onto the cobbled streets of my alleyway. No zombies around that I can see as immediately threatening.

Wait! There's one! And it's good and rotting. Probably dead for a while before the outbreak, as his or her face is almost completely rotted off. It still has eyes though, which are hooked into me and surely thinking 'food.'

You best think again, I think to myself, and bring the machete down hard on its head, severing it completely in half at the jaw, which sends a cloud of dust everywhere. The half jaw squirts what I assume is congealed blood. I'm not sure because it's black and oozy. Maybe it's brain matter, perhaps it's a little of both.

I turn, wide-eyed, and look around. First to the left and then the right. No zombies. I turn some more, and face the street. I must get to the main road.

I run fast, sweating profusely from my outfit. I'm going to need water soon. Damn. Still, I bet I look fantastic in my flannel and jeans.

When I reach the main road I see what Erica Riggins meant by the streets being undriveable. 4th Street is clogged with cars, which isn't really that odd, but this time the cars are so close you could walk on them like an elevated road.

I look at the intersection. The Starbucks is on fire. That makes me laugh. Suddenly a car, which has somehow made it down the crowded street, comes to a halt with screeching brakes. It runs over what looks like a little zombie girl in a sundress. I laugh hysterically. Take that, you little zombie bitch! I watch the little girl's body fly into the intersection, where it lands with a wonderful smash on top of a blue Toyota. Ah, it's great to be alive.

I take a deep whiff of the city air, which smells a little bit too much like smoke. I gaze up at the sky. It looks deep tangerine orange, and is filled with doom; it's the exact color from the *Dawn of the Dead 2004* DVD case. The perfect color for the sky to be during a Zombie Apocalypse.

I stand proud for a moment. This is what I've been waiting for my entire life. No one ever understood why I wanted this, but I know why. Equalization has come. The playing field has been leveled out. Those of us who were meant to survive now are going to survive. No more 7-Elevens. No more voting. No more waiting in line at Target for a shower curtain next to some fat lady with body odor who isn't moving because she's reading the plot synopsis of the 'Bratz' DVD. It's every man for himself. Those who are meant to survive will, and those that won't will die, and probably join the undead ranks!

Z-day is here, people! Bring it on!

My thoughts are suddenly interrupted by a severe pain in my stomach, which knocks me to the ground. I let out a terrible scream. It would appear I'm bleeding profusely, as I can see blood spilling all over my wonderful flannel shirt, the plaid becoming wet with blood. Did I get bit? No. It appears I've been shot.

"Oh my God," a voice calls from behind. "I'm sorry, man. I thought you were one of them."

I look up, shocked. It's the homeless man I thought was a zombie. I see now he isn't.

The homeless man leans over me, his eyes panicked. He's covered in blood. My blood. Uh-oh.

The homeless man holds me in his arms.

"I'm so sorry. I thought you were one of them. You were just standing there!"

I smile at him. I don't know why I'm smiling, considering I'm shot. I think I may be losing consciousness.

The homeless man looks around the street.

"I really am sorry, man. I didn't mean it. I thought you were one of them. Oh man, you're bleeding really bad."

I hear more noise in the background. It sounds like bombs. The sky is still orange.

I look the homeless man in the eyes, and then glance behind him. Another zombie, who looks a lot like me, is approaching.

I smile once more at the homeless man and chuckle, "Why the hell don't they make bellbottoms anymore?"

ROUTE Z

PATRICK MACCADOO

The zombie snapped his face toward Clive.

Clive hesitated mid-stride. He fought the impulse to drop the package and bolt back to his mail truck, which was so close he could hear the dulcet tone of Ben Pitt's voice on the radio, as Ben ranted about some wily zombie congressman. Clive knew that the zombie's flesh-starved glare was involuntary.

The zombie, astride a huge green riding-lawnmower, sported a candy-pink pullover and loose khakis. With styled blonde locks and rosy, clean-shaven cheeks, the zombie's grooming was impeccable. Smart zombies were always extra careful about hygiene and attire, so as not to be confused with dumb zombies, or at least the public perception of dumb zombies staggering about in rags, drooling and filthy.

Still, Clive hated that hungry stare. He hated this part of his route. McMansions. Perfect green lawns. Smooth roads and un-cracked sidewalks. Somehow, the sky seemed bluer, and in most backyards, in spite of the law, a tethered dumb-zombie or two. Damned gated communities. He yearned for the days when his biggest worry was runaway dogs.

Clive hurried to the next house and up its stone walkway, which led to a cement ramp wide enough for a half-dozen wheel-chairs. He leaned into the slope, feeling the effort in his calves, and swore for the millionth time that he was gonna drop a few pounds. Forget about heart disease and diabetes. In this era of the zombie, being middle-aged and tubby, and thus slow-footed, was fatal.

The darkened windows gave him a moment of hope that no one would be home, and he could just leave a sticker on the door to prove he tried. He stifled a groan. Behind the screen door, the front door was wide open.

He knocked on the door's wooden frame. Each rap jounced the rickety door open a crack. On the last jounce, a fat black fly buzzed out through the crack. A tremulous voice called, "Come in."

Clive sagged. He didn't know which was worse, brief interactions with smart zombies struggling to show no visible signs of cannibalistic impulses, or the excruciating coaxing of old ladies to sign for packages. Then there were the 'bitties' hemming and hawing over his electronic clipboard, pretending like they'd never seen such a newfangled contraption, even though most of them received at least one package a month.

Clive mumbled, "Damned hazard pay." They fired the last man to work this route because they caught him tossing mailbags into the river. Last Thursday, when he took over, he thought the guy was a lazy moron. Now he could sympathize. The extra pay wasn't worth it. The Glock holstered on his hip did not make him feel safe. But now he was at the mercy of his manager, who would no doubt deny any requests for a transfer, at least until he met the mandatory three-month threshold.

"Package delivery," he said through the screen door.

The old lady called back, "Bring it in, please."

He bristled. These gated-community folk treated him like he was their butler. He considered slapping the sticker on the door and walking away; let her drag her ass down to the main office and pick up her own damn package. But he knew she wouldn't do that. No, she'd call in a complaint. He'd get a black mark on his permanent record, and his manager would have grounds to deny a transfer request.

He stepped inside. The gloom offered no relief from the September heat. He inhaled a nose full of dusty air and sneezed. From the foyer, he peered into the dining room to see a china hutch, a massive oak table, and heavy oak chairs arranged helter-skelter around it. On the table was a breakfast bowl, a spoon handle leaning on its rim, with the cereal box in front of it—childish reading material. He sniffled. A gamy odor pervaded.

Shame welled up in him. If she'd been rich, she wasn't anymore. Any maids or butlers were long gone. She was probably holding on to the place by the skin of her teeth.

"We're in the parlor."

He followed the sound of her voice. Heavy curtains deepened the darkness of the parlor, which was lit by the antique console TV against the far wall. He was a little surprised to see the daytime talk show *Sarah!* was showing in color, and not in black and white.

The hunched old lady sat in an electric wheelchair. Her gnarled hands jittered in her lap, her eyes blinked owl-like behind her thick glasses. On the worn couch, a little blonde girl in a prim blue dress and saddle shoes dangled her feet a few inches above the dusty floor.

"Hello young man," the old lady said.

He couldn't repress a quiet snort at being called 'young.' He nodded his head and said, "Got a package for you, ma'am."

"Just set it on the coffee table."

He went into robot mode, confining his movements to a set of simple tasks, eschewing eye contact and details, the world growing fuzzy as he withdrew deep within himself, drudging his way to the other side of yet another distasteful chore.

He had the digital pen in the old lady's hand, had her on the cusp of signing, when the faint clink of chains from the floor below startled him out of his self-induced torpor. He refocused on the little girl, her glassy eyes, blank expression, and missing left arm.

He blinked. The parlor's gloom could not conceal the slipshod nature of the ragged amputation.

"Egger won't eat anything else," the old lady said. "He's just wasting away, and I'm afraid he'll starve to death before he gets better. They get better, you know, like that nice Mister Glover next door. All he needs is a little more time."

Clive pawed at the snap on his gun holster's leather flap.

"Oh my, I'd hate to have to shoot you, young man," the old lady said calmly.

She pointed a sleek, well-oiled automatic at him, a make he was unfamiliar with, but definitely on the high end. He noticed her hands had lost their palsy, that she seemed comfortable aiming a firearm.

"I'm awful sorry about all this, but I need someone with stronger hands to do the job right. Egger won't eat dead meat, and little Angie here almost died when her arm came off."

"You can't believe you'll get away with this. I'm a mailman!"

"Oh, the neighbors won't like it one bit, but they'll pitch in, they always do." She let loose a dry cackle. "They have no choice." She waved the gun's muzzle toward the package. "Now you'll find surgical instruments in there that'll help you do a good job. Just keep in mind that it behooves you to succeed, because the longer Angie lives, the better chance you have to keep all your own limbs."

Clive looked into the old lady's watery gray eyes. Of course she was insane, had to be to think she could simply imprison him, turn him into her own personal vivisectionist, while feeding a little girl, piece by piece, to the slobbering wreck chained up in the basement, her son, or whatever. He'd heard the rumors of rich people feeding their afflicted family members in just this way.

He narrowed his eyes. "Who is she?"

The old lady worked her jaw. "The maid's daughter."

Clive's eyes darted from side to side. The dust and the disarray suddenly made sense. She'd fed the help to Egger. Angie was all that was left, and desperate to appease her son's appetite for human flesh, she concocted this scheme. He considered going for his Glock, but the old lady's unwavering hand, and the fact she'd been able to murder her servants, convinced him otherwise.

Angie scratched her sloppily-bandaged shoulder. Clive knew he couldn't hack her other arm off, even though his life depended on it. He swayed.

"I need you to surrender your sidearm, dear. Do it just like they do on TV. Pull it out with your forefinger and thumb, then place it on the coffee table."

He unsnapped the holster. He foresaw days, maybe weeks of imprisonment before he could escape. He couldn't help imagining the old lady holding her fancy gun on him, forcing him to saw through Angie's shoulder joint. He could hear the wet sound of bloody flesh tearing, the nerve-grating vibrations of a hacksaw grinding against bone traveling through the saw and into his fingers.

It would be infinitely better to force her to shoot him.

He began to ease his sidearm out of its holster. Her eyes seemed clearer. Looking at her hag's face, he believed she could read his intentions.

There was a loud knock at the front door.

He jumped and jerked the gun halfway out of the holster, his heart in his throat. A runnel of sweat oozed down from the old lady's temple. A slight tremor shook her gun hand.

A male voice called from the foyer, "Dolores, what's going on?"

The old lady licked her cracked lips.

"I'm coming in," the male voice said.

Clive exhaled a shuddering breath as the old lady held the gun on him. A man appeared in the entrance between the parlor and the hallway; it was the lawn-mowing smart zombie. In his pink shirt, the blonde hair, the angry expression, he looked like any other human being.

"Dolores, you know better than this," the zombie said.

Clive didn't like the look in the smart zombie's eyes, it looked too much like he was calculating if he could have a feast and get away with it. "The main office knows I'm here," Clive said.

The smart zombie, his eyes seeming to still calculate the chances of a meal, said, "Relax, friend. Dolores just had a moment of confusion." He leaned toward the old lady. "You get your medications mixed up again, hon? I'll bet that's what it is. Now put that gun down before you hurt someone."

The old lady's head quivered, then her breast hitched, and she lowered the gun to her lap.

"I don't know what got into me." Her voice shook slightly.

The smart zombie patted her arm. "There, there, dear, we'll sort it all out." He straightened and peered at Clive. "You can go." His eyes narrowed. "But you better keep your mouth shut about this."

Clive felt the heat rise into his face. He understood what the smart zombie meant. The rich had a long reach. He was telling Clive that bad things would happen if he reported this incident.

The little girl shifted her gaze to the hardwood floor.

"What about her?" Clive asked about Angie.

The smart zombie shrugged. "Can't let her go, not now."

"Where's her mother?"

The smart zombie raised an eyebrow. "What do you want to hear, friend?" He stared at Clive for a few seconds. "Don't make me change my mind about letting you go."

Clive felt a heaviness behind his eyeballs. He placed his palm on the butt of his sidearm. He pivoted his head so that the girl vanished from his peripheral vision. She already knew he was going to turn his back on her. He pushed his sidearm down, so that it was snug in its holster, then snapped the flap over it. The smart zombie stepped to the side and let Clive pass.

Clive shoved the screen door so hard it slammed against the side of the house. He squinted against the blinding sunshine. The white picket fence flickered in the corner of his eye, the pungency of fresh-cut grass swirling up his nostrils. The slap of his postal-issued shoes on the smooth sidewalk disturbed the street's chirping tranquility as he hurried to his mail truck.

He got into the driver's seat, the vehicle bouncing under his weight. The stately houses up and down the block were dead quiet. How many others were dismembering children a limb at a time in order to feed a zombified relative? He wondered.

He started the engine, backed the vehicle up, and U-turned. He floored it, the speedometer's needle fluttering. He whipped the steering wheel hard and the tires climbed the curb in front f the old lady's house. The truck jostled over the green grass of her manicured lawn. His eyes slitted as the mail truck tilted up the wheelchair ramp, and he closed them as the grille smashed into the rickety screen door and plowed into the home.

Plaster, splintered wood and glass shards rained down, clattering on the mail truck's roof. The engine whined and died and foundational timber groaned.

Clive opened his eyes. Eddies of white dust filled the air. He coughed, then pulled his shirt up to cover his mouth and nose. He jerked his sidearm out of its holster, got out of the mail truck, and headed for the parlor.

The little girl hadn't moved from the couch, her saddle-shoed feet still dangling above the floor. The old lady was lying on her side next to the capsized wheelchair. She thumbed the button on the remote control in her hand over and over, then uttered a thin screech.

Clive spotted the old lady's gun and kicked it into the corner. She screamed at him. He grabbed the little girl, toted her under his left arm, and went back to the mail truck.

He stowed her in the back among the empty mail sacks, then started up the truck and threw it into reverse. It lurched backward. The engine chugged, the vehicle straining, but it didn't gain any ground. He checked his side mirror, miraculously still attached to the vehicle. In the whirling dust, he couldn't see the obstruction, but he could see the sunny blue sky that meant freedom for him and the girl.

He twisted forward while putting the transmission into drive.

A figure emerged from the plaster dust clouds. Coated in white powder, bulging, yellowed eyes blinking, drool dripping viscous from his chin, Clive assumed this was Egger, released from the basement by the old lady's remote control.

Clive aimed his gun at the zombie's head as he squinted against the dust. Underneath the fine white grit, the zombie was wearing a butler's uniform. Clive realized that this poor shmuck was not Egger, but perhaps an early, failed attempt to feed Egger, an experiment that resulted in the zombification of a member of the household staff, the wretch turned into some perverted version of a guard dog.

He re-aimed. There was nothing he could do for the man now. He pulled the trigger and glanced away from the zombie's spastic jerk when bullet met flesh. The clean headshot took the zombie down, where it twitched on the floor for a few seconds before going still.

Clive holstered his gun and wheeled around. More zombies, former maids, drivers, and gardeners—judging by the remains of their ragged clothing—were coming at him. He grabbed the girl, drew the gun again, and hoisted her to his hip. He hurried into the hall, but he could hear their shuffling steps coming from the rear of the house.

He was surrounded!

He found a staircase and tromped up it. As he felt his arrhythmia kick in, he cursed his overweight ass as he gasped for breath. He made it to the upper landing when the first wave of dizziness came over him. As the world turned to static before his eyes, he reeled, gritting his teeth. When the wave passed, he looked downstairs, and the first of the zombies were there, scowling up at him.

He ran into the closest room, a bedroom facing the street. He put the girl down on the bed and slammed the door shut. He pushed a dresser in front of the door, then slumped down with his back to it, his feet sprawled out before him.

He panted, feeling a sick sheen of sweat on his brow. His pulse was rapid and uneven, swelling to bursting then barely a blip, beating erratic.

"Are you all right?" the little girl asked.

He looked up at her and barked a wheezy laugh. "Got a bad ticker, little one. Comes and goes." He gulped in a breath. "Never got it checked out. Guess I didn't want to hear the bad news."

Footsteps clomped on the floorboards outside the door and he felt pressure against his back. He looked around the room for an option. The suggestive gaze of singers and starlets from the past, none of whom he recognized, every single one of them with parted lips, stared back at him from posters on the wall. Egger's room. He spotted a couple of Louisville Sluggers in one corner.

He slid an inch on the floor as the door was pushed open, then dug in his heels and pushed back, regaining the lost ground. He guessed he should've dragged the king-sized bed over when he had the chance. He checked his gun, knowing he couldn't hold them back forever.

His eyes went to the window. He tried to imagine himself jumping out it while holding the little girl, to then land in the soft grass to the side of the cement ramp, without injuring himself to the point he couldn't get up and run.

He coughed up a dry chuckle. There'd be more zombies. Whoever sicced these poor bastards on him would be waiting to unleash more, just in case he escaped. He'd always dismissed the rumors of zombie sports, zombie bouts, zombie hunts, and the rest, as typical blue-collar bashing of the wealthy, but now things looked very different.

The pressure at his back pushed him an inch further. The zombies were weak from hunger, but their numbers would win out. He'd be damned if he'd let them tear into him and the girl, ripping them into bloody pieces.

The best-case scenario was that he and the girl would end up in the undead pack, infected, the playthings for the idle rich. He knew that before he would let that happen, he'd put some of them out of their misery, then save the last two bullets for himself and the girl.

With a grunt he lurched to his feet. The door slammed into his butt as the zombies flooded into the room. He snatched the girl and swung her behind him. He aimed the gun at the nearest zombie. There were so many. The neighbors meant for there to be no leftover traces. They would dispose of his mail truck once he was dead. When the investigators came, *if* they came, the neighbors would give a practiced shrug, and suggest that Clive was just another victim of a random zombie attack. It happened all the time, in the streets outside of their gates.

The floorboards beneath him creaked and he backed the girl up to the window. He dropped the first zombie with a head shot.

Pop, pop, pop, and two more went down, the third bullet slamming into the mob, though he didn't see what it hit. The living dead stumbled over the downed bodies.

He pulled the girl back up to his hip and said, "Hold on, honey." She threw her one arm around his neck. The twenty-five extra pounds kept him from jumping. The floor dropped a few inches, then some more, the lower supports damaged from when his mail truck had driven into the house, taking out structural architecture.

The sound of wood and plaster splitting was like thunder as the floor gave way. He pulled the girl into his embrace, covering her head and hunching over as they fell to the floor below.

The impact rattled his teeth, scrambled his brains. He groaned. Wild, haphazard throbs rioted throughout his body. The girl stirred in his arms.

He got to his feet and reeled among the debris before extending both arms for balance. His right ankle pinged in pain, his left knee balked, but he could still walk on them.

The girl struggled to push herself up, but one-armed, she only managed to flop to her back. A zombie in a disheveled and stained chef's uniform dragged his body, hand over hand, over the shattered wood and plaster chunks toward the girl. Clive's hand slapped his empty holster. He scanned the debris, the askew mattress and box-spring, the splintered dresser, the scattered zombies, most prone and unmoving, a few struggling to rise.

The smart zombie, the neighbor, watched from the safety of his trimmed lawn through the demolished open door. He was sipping a glass of what looked like lemonade. Clive broke eye contact with the asshole and hobbled to the girl. She cried out when he yanked her up by her one arm.

"I'm sorry, honey."

She blinked the tears out of her eyes. He hoisted her to his hip again and sidestepped the crippled zombie. He could see through the opening he'd made with his mail truck that more zombies were coming down the street. He took a moment to stare angrily at the neighbor, who watched the show with impassive eyes while leaning against his big green riding mower and sipping his beverage.

Within the demolished front of the house, the rear bumper of the mail truck reflected the glare of the sun. In between, dazed zombies swayed to their feet. Clive veered out of the debris field and hurried as fast as his damaged right leg would allow to the opposite side of the house. He felt a small measure of relief to be out of the neighbor's eye line, but the exertion, especially toting the girl, got his bum ticker careening again. Tiny electric dizzy-spots bloomed in his field of vision and taking the concrete steps to the back door caused those spots, flashing blue and black, to multiply, the dizziness closing in.

The back door was unlocked. He locked it, put the girl down, and bent over with his palms on his thighs, gasping as he waited for the spell to pass.

The little girl tugged on his shirt and he looked up at her. Through the next doorway he saw a lone zombie in the kitchen. By the pastel orange polo shirt and white nylon sweats, Clive assumed the young zombie was Egger. He wasted a moment wondering how the old lady managed to keep Egger's brown hair feathered and his snapping teeth so blindingly white.

Clive snatched a nine iron out of a golf bag leaning against the wall. Egger paused a few paces from the doorway, as if gauging his next move. A chill went through Clive at the thought that

Egger was smart enough to keep from walking into a beating, but not in control of his appetites. Clive could see that fact in Egger's hungry brown eyes.

Egger's face contorted into a sallow grimace. He shook a fist at Clive, and his voice came out halting and scraping like grinding gears, yet somehow preserving a strain of privilege. "Get…your *filthy* hands…off my golf club."

Clive snapped the nine iron on Egger's kneecap in reply. As Egger yelped, Clive slid another club out of the bag.

"Nice sticks. You back up now, or I'll break 'em all," Clive said. He suppressed his shock that Egger actually backed up, both hands out, his eyes bulging, his starving rage plummeting into helpless pleading. "Get back!"

Egger circled backwards around the kitchen table., "They…won't…let you go." His grinding voice made Clive wince.

"So what am I supposed to do? Give up? Let you bastards eat me, eat *her*, one inch at a time?"

"I have…money."

Clive shook in anger. He wasn't sure if the zombie was taunting him, or offering him a bribe, and he wasn't sure which upset him more.

A strained whirring grew louder, filling the house. Suddenly, in the doorway beyond Egger, emerging from the gloom of the hallway, the old lady, astride a metallic-red power chair, burst screaming into the kitchen, one claw gripping the handlebars, the other her gun, which she leveled at Clive.

He dove to the linoleum, pulling the girl with him. Shots popped, bullets clanging off the hanging pots and pans, thudding into the walls. There was a thump and the kitchen table was sliding towards him. He crawled as fast as he could, the table's legs clipping his ankles before it smashed into the wall, and a *whump* shook the floor.

The continuous bleat of the power chair's horn filled the kitchen. Clive bent down and grabbed the side of the power chair, then lifted with everything he had. As it flipped over, he stumbled a few paces before getting his legs squared beneath him. Not stopping there, he flipped the table on her as well.

The tipped-over power chair squashed the splayed, motionless body of the old lady. One edge of the heavy oak table had crushed the old lady's breastbone, and the other edge was flush against the far wall, the table's ramp-like tilt sparing him the sight of the old lady's death mask.

Egger held the girl over by the door to the back porch. Clive didn't see the old lady's gun among the overturned chairs. He met Egger's yellowed gaze while sidling closer to the hallway. He glimpsed his mail truck. The ruined front of the house was still clear of zombies, but smelling fresh meat, they were sure to worm through the wreckage. By now, every starving zombie in the neighborhood would be slouching toward the house. Once they started to get inside, there would be no hope of escape.

Egger clutched the little girl's hand. His gaze turned cocky, knowing that the threat of infection was enough to keep Clive at arm's length.

Clive shifted closer to the hallway. The mail truck was only a short dash away. He couldn't be sure, but when he caught a glimpse of the collapsed front of the house, the jittery vision insisted that whatever had obstructed the truck from backing out had fallen free as the debris settled. The unimpeded shafts of sunlight illuminating the far end of the hall added support to his belief. Finally, a wriggly whisper from the deep dark of his mind urged him to go now; he could make it but he had to go *right now*.

He lowered his eyelids to slits, only seeing the hallway, blurring the rest of the world. He'd done some bad things in his life. He had a list. He hoped everyone had a list of things they wished they'd done differently. Before, he was able to convince himself that maintaining such a list kept him out of the sociopath category. But if he did this; if he ran way, abandoned her, left the girl to die.

He lowered his eyelids further until his lashes created a meshed veil. He was old enough to remember how certain sickos used to love zombie movies. Hell, he'd watched a few. He remembered the scenes where zombies cornered victims and tore them to shreds. Awful, sure, but at least it was a quick death.

He'd read Adam Meyer's Pulitzer-winning series dealing with his personal ordeal of zombification, focusing on the horror of the transformation from dumb to smart zombie, the nigh-overwhelming craving for human flesh warring against the rising awareness of the atrocity of cannibalism. And he'd seen the Dateline shows, the ones with the remorseful teenagers, formerly thrill-seekers, who got caught up in the fad of getting 'zombed.'

A wet sniffle jolted him. His eyes popped open, dispelling his artificial myopia. Egger clutched her one hand. Her head was bowed. Tracks from tears running through the dust covering her face glistened on her cheeks. No, not 'the girl.' Her name was Angie. Her silent weeping suggested that perhaps, this whole damned time, she wasn't suffering shock, she wasn't near catatonic, but rather she was deeply resigned to her fate.

"Oh hell," Clive muttered.

He snatched up one of the solid wooden chairs and whipped it at Egger's head as he ran at the zombie, then he shoved the power chair off the corpse and spotted the gun on the floor. Angie was pushed out of the way when Egger let her go, protecting himself from the chair.

Clive lunged for the gun but his attempt deteriorated into an awkward stumble and he kicked the gun with his foot, which skittered across the linoleum and clattered into Egger's shoes. Clive redirected his doddering momentum towards the upended table and drove it up and into Egger.

The table slammed into the wall, the sudden stop jarring Clive to his knees. He got up but a gunshot made him duck back down. He twisted down on his butt, his back against the overturned table top. Clive imagined Egger preparing to shoot on the other side, imagined the punch of bullets through oak before entering his fatty backside.

A small hand touched his jaw and there she was, like a little one-armed angel. With a long, growling grunt, he rose to his feet and lifted her to his hip. He hobbled toward the hall, waiting to feel a bullet hit his back. He couldn't muster any extra energy for evasive maneuvers, couldn't even muster the energy to think of one. He staggered down the hallway, the gloom giving way to rays of sunshine.

He chose to focus on the bright warmth, rather than the undead swarm clustering outside and the half-smart zombie pointing a gun at him. He ducked into the mail truck and placed the girl among the bags in the rear. He plopped into the driver's seat.

"C'mon, old girl," he whispered as he turned the key. "Start." After a brief grinding, the engine hummed to life. He threw it into reverse.

The tires rolled an inch, then stopped. He goosed the gas pedal, and the engine whined, then the back end rocked up and over something, the rear tires grabbing the floor, the truck battering through the wreckage. Zombies thumped off the sides as the truck sped down the ramp and skidded across the debris-strewn lawn.

When Clive reached the street, he stomped the brakes while whipping the steering wheel hard to the left. The tires squealed, the momentum scattering the contents within. Angie yipped loudly, and as Clive put the transmission into drive, he could've sworn her yip sounded a little like the delighted shrieks of children zooming down a roller coaster.

Clive stepped on the gas pedal and the engine sputtered then evened out. He saw the neighbor, standing in the middle of his lush green lawn, watching intently. The neighbor shrugged. Clive shifted his gaze to the road and drove away. There was nothing the neighbor could do now, except call the security guard at the gate.

A minute later, he exhaled a hot, relieved breath when he saw the wide open gate. His heart felt like a superball ricocheting off his breastbone, it was beating so fast, and he took deep breaths in the effort to slow it. When he passed the security booth, he nodded at the gatekeeper, just another working shmuck, who returned his nod, then went back to reading his magazine.

Clive glanced in the rearview mirror. The gates were slowly closing, still no zombies in sight. Angie crawled into the space next to his seat and blinked her big baby blues at him. Looking at her messily-bandaged arm, he guessed the next stop was the hospital.

"God I hate Mondays," he said.

She giggled.

THE FINAL PERFORMANCE

MATT KURTZ

Exactly forty-two days into the apocalypse, Sarah became one of undead.

Since it began, she had been hiding alone in her house behind boarded windows and doors while the legion of reanimated roamed the neighborhood, hungry for the flesh of the living. The electricity had been out for the past month, and even with all her careful rationing, her supply of water, canned goods, and candles were nearly depleted. With it being too dangerous to venture outside to scrounge for more supplies, she knew her survival was only an exercise in futility.

Life was cruel like that.

Such as the day the batteries died on her portable radio, denying her a final glimmer of hope. Up until then, she listened to the voices over the airwaves announcing that a makeshift shelter might be set up by a band of survivors on the outskirts of town. She knew the exact location of the planned establishment, but never found out whether it was actually put into effect after the batteries went dead. That was over three weeks ago.

Life was beyond cruel. It downright sucked.

She never had the chance to marry. Have children. Or more importantly, at least to her, become the famous stage and screen actress she had aspirations for since childhood.

She guffawed, thinking of all the money wasted on classes that taught her how to entertain and captivate an audience that now ceased to exist in this undead world.

Cheated of the opportunity to give a single, great performance, she accepted that the curtain had drawn on the play of life and it was time to take her final bow.

Yes, indeed. Life sucked.

She prepared herself to do what needed to be done. Staring at her candlelit reflection in the vanity's mirror, she fingered the .38 caliber pistol sitting next to her jars of makeup and brushes. She inhaled deeply and nodded.

There was no other option. It was time.

An hour after a single gunshot shattered the silence of the neighborhood, Sarah stirred within the house.

When the front door swung open, the near dozen zombies in the yard whirled in the direction of the movement. They groaned and shuffled to the front porch with arms raised.

Then paused.

Sarah stood in the open doorway, her eyes glazed over and her once tan skin now bleached white in a marbled complexion. Her hair was horribly matted with blood from the exit wound on top of her head.

With one hand tightly balled into a fist, the other was clutching the gun in a death grip. She responded with a groan of her own and drooled blood from where the pistol had been inserted only an hour earlier.

The zombies studied her, then turned away, uninterested in the new arrival. Her feet slid forward and she stumbled off the porch and down the steps. Shuffling to the driveway, she passed Mrs. Kincaid, the old widow from two houses down. For a brief moment, they seemed to lock eyes in slight recognition. The old dead woman was the first to look away, her attention shifting to the door left ajar on the front porch.

Sarah shambled across the lawn to her Volvo still parked in the driveway. A few feet from the vehicle, a bloated mailman, gnawing on the hind leg of a large dog, stepped in front of her. Sarah slowed to a stop. Ripping a furry piece of flesh from the leg bone, the mailman appeared to be smiling between his chews. Maybe in this upside down world, it was a little slice of poetic justice for the suffering he'd endured at the paws of all the non-tethered canines along his route.

Once the mail courier lumbered past her, Sarah's unblinking eyes shifted back and forth. Her clenched fist relaxed, allowing the key ring to drop. The automatic clicker to the Volvo's locks swung back and forth like a pendulum until her forefinger and thumb clamped over it.

Her finger twitched, pushing one of the buttons. The locks on the door popped up.

A few of the living dead cocked their heads in the direction of the sound. Before they could fully turn and move closer, Sarah lunged forward and yanked open the driver's door, diving inside.

The zombies spun to face the car.

Slamming the door shut, Sarah tossed the pistol on the passenger seat. She slid the key in the ignition and fired up the engine, thanking God the battery still had some juice left in it. The undead moved to surround the Volvo as the engine revved and the reverse lights lit up.

Screeching tires echoed into the night.

As Sarah sped down the residential street, swerving around the living dead and the smoldering debris in the road, she glanced in the rearview mirror at her ghastly appearance and laughed hysterically. If her theatrical makeup instructor, Mr. Belsic, was still alive, she would have hugged him for being such a damn good teacher!

A half hour later, she stopped on the rural road leading to the shelter mentioned on the radio. She checked the darkness surrounding the car for any movement then put the transmission into park. After noticing the lights in the distance behind a thicket of trees, she breathed a sigh of relief. Her gamble had paid off.

You did it. You made it, she thought.

Smiling, she looked in the rearview mirror to congratulate herself. Her eyes widened at her undead reflection.

Uh-oh. Ya better wipe off the greasepaint before they think you're one of them.

The driver's side window exploded and half of Sarah's head blew apart. Brain and skull fragments splattered the car's interior. Her body slumped onto the passenger seat.

Two men cloaked in camouflage and clutching rifles stepped from the shadows on the side of the road. They approached the vehicle and opened its door, staring inside at the crumpled driver.

"Holy shit!"

"Told ya it was one of 'em."

"I can't believe they've figured out how to drive."

"Better call it in so they can send a warning over the short-wave. People better know that the puss heads are evolving."

After pushing the Volvo off the road, the men returned to their sentry post to continue guarding the shelter from any outside threats. Especially from the undead that were now, apparently, remembering certain things.

RAGE AGAINST THE DEAD

DARREN WJ MILLS

Just as the clock struck five o' clock in the morning, John realized he'd been awake for nearly ten minutes and his usual Monday morning routine was due to start in just over an hour.

One too many glasses of wine before dragging himself off to bed had caused his bladder to swell shortly after he'd fallen asleep and now, three and half hours later, he was awake with the feeling his bladder was ready to explode.

After the initial pain John had felt building up around his genital area, he attempted to drag his half-asleep body out from under his extremely warm and cozy duvet. The cold air that always settled around the house during the night hit his bare skin like a wall of pins, sending him scuttling back under the protection of the duvet and towards whatever warmth he could steal from Carol, his girlfriend.

Soon, his eyes adjusted to the dark within the bedroom and he could now make out the features on Carol's face. He could see from the sweat across her brow and the dampness on her pillow that she was no better off than before going to bed.

Carol had gone to bed hours before John and fallen asleep almost immediately. Their weekend had been a busy one, consisting of a strenuous amount of DIY in the house they had only been living in for the last two weeks. Saturday had been dedicated to stripping wall paper, while Sunday was the day for putting up new lining paper to get ready for fresh paint.

Although Saturday went by without any problems, Sunday was almost the complete opposite. Neither John nor Carol had ever been any good at the whole decorating game. So after many failed attempts at getting the wall paper to stick to the wall with no lumps or bumps, they decided to give up and take a walk to the local shop to buy some well deserved wine and relax for the evening.

Their trip to the shop was fine on the way there. There was no sign of any other soul around and the shop was completely empty apart from themselves and the shopkeeper. All was quiet until they crossed the road opposite the shop and began their five minute walk home.

John sighed in his bedroom and leaned over Carol, feeling her head as she lay almost completely still. She had made groaning noises with occasional squints of pain showing across her face while he was awake, but for all he knew she'd been like that all night.

Her forehead was ice cold but it was covered in sweat. John quickly pulled himself out from under the warm duvet covers and grabbed his dressing gown off the chair at the end of the bed.

Although the cold air around the room was still sending shivers down his spine, his worry for Carol, on top of the fact his bladder was almost ready to burst, was enough for him to easily brave the cold and make the journey to the toilet.

As he crossed the hallway and entered the toilet opposite the bedroom, he began muttering under his breath and shaking his head in anger at the events that had occurred during their walk home from the shops.

"Stupid, so bloody stupid."

After buying their two bottles of wine from the shop, they had crossed the road opposite, almost running, eager to get home, but John ended up tripping over from an untied shoelace. He hadn't hurt himself but he did end up stopping to tie the lace. Carol however, was too eager to crack on with their much needed wine drinking session and carried on walking, taunting him as she increased speed.

But as she progressed further and further, getting far enough along to turn the first corner, she was met with a terrible sight.

John heard his girlfriend scream out in pain after beginning to walk again and instantly broke out into a sprint, scared by the fear and pain he heard in her voice, and desperate to get to her aid.

As he turned the same corner she'd disappeared around moments before, he almost let out a scream himself, horrified by the sight. Carol had been knocked to the ground and was pinned by a man on top of her, trying to bite at her face. His clothes were dirty and torn, with blood dripping from his mouth. John had been quick to act by grabbing the man by the collar of his coat and yanking him off Carol, sending him tumbling to the side.

As he pulled Carol onto her feet, he immediately saw she was badly cut across the wrist, with blood almost pumping out.

Before he had the chance to cringe in horror at the sight and comfort her, the man who attacked her was on his feet again and was now making his way back for more.

It only took a couple of seconds for John to lose all control over his temper and send the man tumbling back to the ground. Instead of stopping there, and leaving the man be, he was unable to control the anger that often built up inside him and had seen him fired from so many jobs over the years.

He began kicking the man where he lay, stamping down on his head, tearing chunks of flesh off his face with every kick.

It was only Carol's pleading screams that stopped John from going too far and killing the man. She'd often seen him lose his temper over the simplest of things and knew he had trouble controlling how far he would go. Although she was sickened by what the man did to her, she would never want to see him killed for it.

Finished in the bathroom, John leaned against the door in the toilet, the pain from his bladder now gone. It was now replaced with a thumping pain in his head. He'd gone too far with the man, almost killing him where he lay. Like always, he'd let his temper get the better of him and because of that, Carol was now suffering.

He thought about the many counseling sessions he'd been to over the years, sessions he arranged with the hope of getting a deeper understanding of where his anger came from and developing a way of controlling it. But those thoughts just made his head pound harder as he recalled the many assault charges brought against him for attacking various counselors who delved too deep. He began banging his head against the toilet door, desperate to mask some of the pain deep inside his mind.

After John had dragged himself away from beating Carol's attacker, he wanted to get her help, to call the police and an ambulance to the scene, and get her the help she needed, but she didn't let him.

He'd badly beat her attacker and Carol knew if they stayed anywhere near the scene, he would definitely be arrested for what he did.

They were lucky that no one was around to see what happened. No one had come out to help, or there would have been witnesses to say John had gone too far.

Instead of getting help, Carol had forced John to run away from the blood-soaked man and go back to their house. Although John had gone along with her plan at the scene of the incident, he still wanted to get her to the hospital after getting home, but she continued to try and protect him by not going anywhere for medical attention. She was too worried they would be connected to the man they had left moaning and bleeding in the road.

John continued to bang his head against the toilet door, not only trying to cover some of the pain from his memories but also to try and release some of the anger he could feel building up in his body. He had vivid images of what he'd done flashing through his mind along with images of the pain he'd seen on Carol's face when she tried to stop the bleeding on her arm.

She finally stopped the blood from pumping out of her wrist hours later, but the pain continued all night long, right up until she went to bed.

She wanted him to go to bed with her but the adrenaline pumping through his body was too intense for him to even think about sleeping. It took four hours and two bottles of wine for him to eventually calm down enough to even attempt to sleep.

As John opened the toilet door, he stopped dead in his tracks. The landing was dark as before and his eyes were still trying to adjust, but he could see that Carol was standing a few feet ahead of him, just inside their bedroom door. As he opened his mouth ready to apologize, realizing he'd woken her by banging his head on the door, she let out a loud moaning sound.

She lurched forward awkwardly, her arms reaching out, her mouth open, almost as if to start biting him. John stood motionless, unable to take in what she was doing; he was no longer angry about his behavior but was instead confused by Carol's actions.

As she made contact with him, John couldn't help staggering backwards and falling to the floor, hitting his head hard against the wall at the end of the corridor and nearly knocking himself unconscious. As he hit the floor, he felt Carol fall on top of him.

He immediately grabbed Carol under her throat, realizing she was about to bite down into his face. His mind couldn't take in what she was doing but his defensive instincts were still very much aware.

"Carol, what the hell are you doing? Get off me!"

He was filled with shock, pain, and a building anger. He could feel tears beginning to well up at the corners of his eyes as he focused on her face.

Her soft, rosy complexion was gone, her complexion now pale, her lips almost gray with small bits of blood filling the cracks in the skin.

"Carol, please…stop!"

John could feel his uncontrollable anger building up in his body as Carol showed no recognition to his voice. Her hands were almost clawing at his face as he tried his hardest to keep her teeth from biting into his flesh.

He couldn't understand what was going on, he didn't want to hurt her but he'd had enough. She'd gone crazy and was trying to kill him, his mind not able to deal with the situation anymore. He felt anger swell throughout his muscles and give him enough strength to roll her weight to one side and push her off with ease.

Unfortunately, he didn't realize how close he was to the top of the stairs, and he actually sent her toppling down them, her body finishing in a motionless heap across the bottom landing.

John rested his head on the floor; his eyes were blurry and his head was throbbing from hitting the wall. Everything from earlier was terrible but what just happened was unimaginable. Carol had attacked him and he'd killed her. He closed his eyes for a moment, taking in deep breaths, almost hoping when he opened his eyes again he would be back in his bed. Carol would be there beside him and everything that happened would be only a nightmare.

Before he could open his eyes, he heard moaning coming from the bottom of the stairs. As he turned his head and tried to focus his blurred vision, he saw Carol back on her feet and awkwardly walking up the stairs towards him.

He slowly got to his feet, taken aback by the sight. Not only was she still alive after such a bad fall, but her left arm was bent the wrong way, with a bone protruding through her forearm. He retched at the sight of her broken body. The sudden anger he felt moments ago was draining away, to be slowly replaced with shock and fear.

Carol was almost at the top of the stairs now and only seconds away from being in biting distance of him again.

"What? How? I don't…oh God…no!"

John wanted nothing more than to rush to Carol and pull her broken body into his arms, but the woman before him was no longer the person he loved. As she reached forward and her soulless eyes glared in the partial light that was beginning to emanate from the night becoming day, John once again felt his uncontrollable anger beginning to flow through his body.

Only this time it wasn't due to the feelings of hate at being attacked, but instead because of what he was being forced to do. Before Carol could get any closer, he lifted his right leg high in the air and kicked out as hard as he could. As his foot made contact with her chin, Carol's head lurched backwards and a loud snapping sound came from her neck. As if in slow motion, John watched her lifeless body hurtle down the stairs, her bones breaking as she hit each step before slumping to a stop at the bottom. This time she didn't get up.

Numb from what he'd just done, he slowly walked down the stairs. He walked passed Carol's body, picked up his mobile phone, pulled his door keys off a hook in the hallway, and unlocked the front door.

He opened the door, walked outside, and began taking in deep lungfuls of the fresh morning air, hoping the shivers running through his body would dissipate with every exhaled breath.

As he punched 9-9-9 into his phone and raised it to his ear, he still couldn't comprehend what just happened, but he knew he needed to answer for his actions.

He sat on the first step of his front porch, his mind full of confusion, but although he couldn't stop playing the last five minutes over and over in his mind, he couldn't help but take notice of various people walking along the street.

There were only four of them but they all took notice of him and were now coming in his direction. Before John's brain could take in the fact that the emergency number he was trying to call was engaged, he focused on the three men and one woman that were just about to enter his front garden. Each of them had been somehow badly disfigured and they were all covered in blood.

John stood up straight and dropped his phone on the ground, not flinching once as it smashed into multiple pieces after making contact with the concrete.

Before the lead man could reach him, John was able to take in various sounds coming from around the neighborhood. He could hear faint screams coming from all directions and in the distance, he could just hear the wail of police sirens.

His mind began working overtime and he remembered about the man from earlier. How he had looked and acted, the fact that he'd bitten Carol and then she went on to act the same way. John could now see that something serious was going on, something big, something he still couldn't fully understand. Before the four disfigured and groaning people could get their hands on him, John turned around, stepped back into his house, and slammed the door. As he turned the lock, he jumped backwards from the sound of the people outside banging on the door, groaning with every hit.

John kept his view away from Carol's body as he ran up the stairs to his bedroom to get dressed. His thoughts now were for his ex-wife Beth and their thirteen-year-old son, Andy. While he'd been in the mind set that what happened moments ago had been secluded to just him and Carol, he hadn't considered how the repercussions would affect his ex-wife and son, but after seeing and hearing what was going on outside, and still hearing the noise coming from his front garden, he knew he had to get to them.

Somehow he had to force his mind to overcome what he'd lost and find a way to get to the people he still had left.

Beth hadn't properly spoken to John ever since she found out he was cheating on her with Carol. But although she hated him for what he did to her and still did now, she knew that Andy meant more to him than anything, and their son was the only person John would never lose his temper with, making him a completely different man when he was around Andy.

Andy also doted on his father, so when the situation of Beth and Andy moving further into the country or staying in the same town, had cropped up many years ago due to work reasons, she immediately put the emotional well-being of her son ahead of her own and decided to stay in a home only a few miles away from John's.

By the time John got dressed and finally gathered all his thoughts about what to do, it was past six o' clock. As he made his way down the stairs, he began cursing to himself for dropping his mobile phone outside. He and Carol had only lived in the house a short while, and the mobile was the only working phone they had, which meant he now had no way of warning Beth about what could happen to her.

He walked past Carol's bloodied body and looked at her one last time. He felt such pain for what happened to her as he stood staring, but his muscles also shivered with anger with every bang he heard coming from the front door.

He wanted to yank open the door and rip through the four people pounding at the glass, making them pay for his loss, but after his encounter with Carol, he had no intention of facing the things alone. He was too worried about the changes that occurred in Carol happening to him if he was infected or whatever was going on.

Before he left, he grabbed a blanket out of the hall closet and covered Carol with it, brushing her hair off her face as he did so. It was the best he could do with him so short on time.

He made his way through the house and let himself out the back door and into the rear garden. As he did this, he couldn't help thinking that if Carol hadn't changed in the night, he would still be in bed with her, oblivious to what was happening, and he would have gotten up as normal and made his way to work without ever realizing anything was amiss.

He'd never paid much attention to others while walking to work, so he knew he probably wouldn't have even registered their strange appearance and behavior until it was too late.

He wondered how many other people were like that right now, unaware of what strange event was happening as they got ready for work, school or to go for a jog.

After climbing his back fence and making his way down the road, John made sure to pay extra attention to his surroundings, very aware he could be attacked at any time. He began to feel sick with shock and fear at every person he saw that was clearly no longer normal.

He could see bloodied men, women and children slowly appearing from multiple doorways and alleyways, almost as if he was letting off some kind of locater alarm and they were desperately responding to it.

After a few more steps, he stopped walking. He shook his head, refusing to take in what his eyes registered ahead of him.

It was the man from the previous day, the man that had made Carol change into a flesh-hungry creature. He was with five other badly mutilated people. They were all kneeling down on the ground, moaning almost in delight at what they'd caught, like they were wild animals.

A body was lying on the ground between them. It was the body of what used to be an elderly woman. John put a hand to his mouth, retching at the sight. The woman had pieces of flesh missing from all over her body. The things were tearing chunks of muscle and fat away from her limbs and feeding on them like they were award winning pieces of meat.

John retched again but this time he couldn't stop himself from throwing up through his fingers and emptying his stomach onto the pavement. As he looked up, he saw that the six men feasting on the woman had heard him and were now looking straight at him.

He could see in the rising morning light that their eyes were fixated on him. He wanted revenge for what the man had done to Carol but he felt no rage building up inside, he knew he needed to escape. There were too many to fight alone.

He quickly turned away from the bloodied men and began running as fast as he could in the opposite direction, desperate to reach Beth and Andy. This was the first time in his life he'd been faced with a situation where he wanted to hurt someone, but his anger hadn't consumed him. Instead, the anger and rage had been replaced with something else—complete and utter fear.

Something terrible had happened to the world, something he just couldn't understand…and he was terrified.

YELLOW GOES TO YELOW, RED GOES TO RED

KELLY M. HUDSON

There was a time of peace after the first Great Rising. It was a relatively short-lived period of about two years. The living dead, beaten back and ultimately brought under control, became the servants of humanity, put to work doing menial tasks.

Society, nearly collapsed from the Great Rising, was suddenly back on its feet again. Infrastructure was rebuilt by a tireless zombie workforce and new laws were instrumented to further the development of the living dead. Interesting new ideas and concepts were evaluated, all geared towards how the dead could help mankind.

This is not a story about that time period, but rather a tale of the end of it. This is about how, despite the machinations of mankind, the Second Great Rising eventually occurred.

And it all began in a tiny little post office in the outskirts of Monkey's Paw, Kentucky.

Watching Dummy move the mail from the right slot to the left, Gerry shook his head. A cigarette danced at the edge of his lip, threatening to fall off and spark on the linoleum floor. It never did, and the trick was one Gerry was quite proud of. Sometimes folks asked him how he did it and he'd smile and tell them it wasn't anything. And it really wasn't. He simply wet the bottom of the filter on the cigarette before he stuck it on his lip. It held like glue.

Right now, though, he wasn't thinking about his cigarette. He was thinking about Dummy and what a stupid bastard he was.

"No, no!" Gerry shouted, waving his arms. Dummy moaned and turned around. He wished Travis had gotten a model with its stupid voice box taken out. But Government grants only went so far, and Dummy was better than the other zombies he had working in the mail room.

Not that he'd ever let Travis know that. Travis was a douche.

Gerry was five and a half feet tall, with reddish-blonde hair, thin and wispy, that blew around his head like a pile of tumbleweeds. He was smallish of build and slight of strength, but he had a meanness about him that made him hell in a fight. He wasn't a quitter, and he'd knock heads with anyone, no matter their size.

He jabbed his finger in Dummy's weathered face. Dummy's jaws moved open and closed, like the dumb zombie was thinking about taking a bite of his finger. Gerry hated that. No matter what they did when they trained them down in Florida, they still acted like they wanted to eat you.

He waved the finger in Dummy's face to get his attention and motioned to the letters in the zombie's hands. He pointed at the yellow sticker on the one letter and the red on the other.

"Yellow goes to yellow," Gerry said. His finger went from the yellow sticker on the paper to the yellow sticker on the side of the slot where the envelope went. "Red goes on red, you idiot." He did the same for the red sticker on the letter and the slot. "Don't they teach you anything down there?"

Dummy moaned and turned back to his work. He placed the yellow-stickered envelope in the yellow-stickered slot. He put the red one in the red one, groaning the entire time. Dummy was six feet tall but stooped. He was bald, like all the zombies, because their dead hair attracted lice and all sorts of unsavory creatures, and that made them unfit to keep around humans. His domed head gave him the appearance of Nosferatu, from that old movie, seeing as his face was narrow, with a pointed chin and nose. His brown eyes were dead, just like the rest of him, although he saw just fine. His skin, dried and tight on his bones, was also a deep brown.

Travis slipped up behind Gerry and slapped his shoulder hard. Travis was forty years old, had thin legs and arms, wore thick eyeglasses, and had a barrel chest that made him look like

Humpty-Dumpty. He didn't like Gerry much, regarding him as a little too redneck for his tastes. But that's the way the world went after the Great Rising. A lot more rednecks than civilized people lived through it because they were simply better armed and meaner than most intellectuals or liberals. The strongest survived, it was always said and staring at Dummy, Travis wondered about all that.

"How's our boy doing today?" Travis asked. He was Gerry's boss. Both men were new to the postal service, Travis having been a businessman before the Great Rising and Gerry being a shiftless layabout. But there was a call for a Post Office in this region of Kentucky, and when Uncle Sam pointed his finger at Travis, he accepted. He'd run a successful hardware store up in Lexington, after all; how hard could a Post Office be to run?

Plenty, it turned out. Most of the internet went down when the dead rose. It crashed and burned and although there were enough people left to fix it, those people were too busy at work trying to figure out more important things, like how to get safe drinking water to certain areas, and how to train zombies to work. The phone system fell apart, too. Cell towers were either knocked down or were now useless, and the regular phone lines were mostly used by Military and Government agencies. That left people with the option of waiting for the internet and the cell phones to get back up and running, or to do it the old way by mailing letters.

Oh, and the letters came. By the thousands. Even through a little crap town like Monkey's Paw.

"I don't know, Boss," Gerry said. He hated calling Travis 'Boss,' but that's what the man wanted. As far as he was concerned, there was only one Boss, and he wasn't named Travis and he wasn't some Jew singer from New Jersey, either.

God was Boss.

"He's better than the others, but hell, he still kinda sucks," Gerry said. He puffed on his cigarette, a plume of smoke jetting from his nostrils.

Travis hated Gerry smoking, but he let his employees have a little latitude on the job. That's why employees loved him and loved to call him Boss, and even though Travis didn't like Gerry, he was pretty sure Gerry liked him.

They had a workforce of ten zombies and four humans. The humans answered the phones and did all the thinking work. The zombies did the grunt work. They sorted the mail. They pushed carts full of packages and letters. They took out the garbage. They did what they were told to do or they got shocked.

The Shockers. It was a small device placed inside the base of the skull of every zombie who'd gone through Government Conditioning in Florida. It sent a zap up into what was left of the functioning parts of a zombie's brain. Travis didn't understand all the science of it, but what little he did made sense to him.

The dead, when they came back, still had nerves and semi-active brains. The brains worked on an instinctual level, almost primitive but not quite. The brains also had active pleasure and pain areas. From what the scientists theorized, eating human flesh somehow stimulated the pleasure region. Nothing touched the pain region, seeing as how their nerves were dead, until they figured out they could operate on them and put the Shockers into the pain area. Now all you had to do was press a button on your Government-issued remote and the zombies would fall to their knees, effectively immobilized.

It helped them to learn, too. The scientists found out early on that zombies responded to pain quicker than pleasure. When it came to the stick or the carrot, zombies worked better by the stick.

Which all made Travis kind of sad. Other than the fact they wanted to eat him, he always felt kind of sorry for the zombies. How would he like it, dying and coming back, only to be hounded and persecuted? And now, when the dead came back, they were sent to Florida for the implanting of the Shockers and re-education. But only those without families left. Those with families were given the choice of cremation or a funeral service. The single ones were rounded up by the National Guard and shipped off. In a clever idea, the Government made sure that whatever area of the country the zombie came from, he or she was never sent back there to work. It was an effort to keep the living from accidentally stumbling on someone they knew.

"I just wish they'd taken out his damn voice box," Gerry said.

Travis smiled.

Gerry hated when he smiled. It was so smug and condescending.

Travis slapped Dummy on the shoulder like he did Gerry.

"Well, Dummy here's a top of the line product, my friend," Travis grinned. "Oh, he's got the base model features. They took out his teeth and his tongue and they chopped off the ends of his fingers, from the last knuckles out. But on the newer models, they torched the ends of the fingers. No more dripping pus, not like with the first line. They also implanted those tiny mints in the gums so that whenever Dummy opens his mouth, out comes a blast of fresh breath, not the usual rot we get with the others."

"Don't those run out?" Gerry asked. He'd smelled Dummy's breath and he didn't recall it being particularly fresh or inviting.

"We have a year's supply, and ordering replacements is cheap," Travis laughed. "Yes, sir, Dummy here is top of the line. Top of the line. Only the best for my Post Office."

"Uh-huh," Gerry said. He was all out of conversation. He wanted Travis to go away and leave him alone. "Okay, Boss. I got it from here."

Travis smiled at Gerry again. He knew his employees liked it when he smiled. Being positive went a long way. Even now, he could tell Gerry was trying to get him to stick around and be a pal, but Travis had work to do. Plus, it wasn't good to mingle too much with the help. It made them think they were on the same level as he was. And excuse him for living, but he used to own his own hardware store. What had Gerry ever done?

"I'll be in my office if you need me," Travis said. He clapped Gerry on the shoulder and sauntered off, pleased with himself.

Gerry stared after him, glad the idiot was gone.

In the back room, one of the other zombies, a tall, skinny one they'd named Paul, stopped pushing his cart and staggered in place, not moving anymore.

Gerry rolled his eyes. "Moron." He fingered the small, black plastic piece on his key ring. It was about the size of an old half-dollar coin and had a bright red button in the middle of it. It was the Shocker remote. He strolled over to Paul and pointed it at him, pressing the button once.

Paul vibrated all over, his dull gray eyes popping out of his sockets for an instant. He moaned and went back to pushing the cart.

That's how the Shockers worked. If you wanted to get one zombie in particular, you pointed at it and tapped the button once. The device sent a concentrated signal in that one direction. You tapped the button twice and the signal went in every direction, zapping all the zombies in the vicinity.

Gerry hummed an old tune and puffed on his dangling cigarette. He thought it was creepy having the zombies around like this, but he sure enjoyed giving them a jolt now and then.

Back over by the sorting slots, Dummy went about his work. He didn't think too often and when he did, it wasn't about much. He knew he was hungry all the time, and that dinner was only inches away, but he couldn't seem to do anything about it. He knew pain, whenever they pressed that button, but that was all.

Except every now and then, something would fire in his brain and he'd get flashes of images, like lightning, and he'd remember things from his life before. They came and went quickly and most times, he forgot them almost immediately. Sometimes, though, the images lingered.

He did remember one, of a little girl on a swing. She wore a bright yellow dress, and had long blonde hair done in pigtails that ran past her shoulders. She giggled like it was going out of style.

He saw his hands how they'd been when he was alive, pushing her, sending her swinging higher and higher, getting more laughter from the happy girl. Then it would fade, go away, and he'd forget. But sometimes he'd remember again and the muscles in his face would almost make him smile.

Jennifer.

The name went through him like a bullet. That was the little girl's name. Jennifer. She'd been his little girl. His daughter. His heart hurt suddenly, a hot pain lancing into it.

Jennifer.

Then he got hungry again and completely forgot what he was thinking. The pang of heartache faded and he moved back to the envelopes. Yellow goes to yellow. Red goes to red. He couldn't forget, or he'd get shocked.

Yellow goes to yellow. Red goes to red.

It was then the two soldiers, Roger and Peter, walked in. They were lanky and white as the President's house. They both had a wide-eyed stare, gawking as they stumbled in, their arms full. They each carried a big brown bag, full to brimming with letters.

Gerry moaned. "God," he muttered, the cigarette still burning on his lip, still hanging on like a jumper who'd re-thought his suicide at the last minute. "The damn military."

They came in once a week. Usually it was two numbnuts like these guys, and they'd have bags full of letters to send to loved ones. Gerry was happy to have a job, but he'd be even happier when they got the phones working again. It would cut this crap in half, easily.

Roger noticed Gerry rolling his eyes and got angry. Who did that redneck think he was, anyway? Treating honest American heroes like him and Peter that way. They were out there every day, on the front lines, keeping everyone safe from the zombie menace. If his mother hadn't taught him manners, Roger might have decided to smack Gerry on the back of the head, just to make an example of him.

Peter didn't care one way or the other. His arms burned from his burden and all he wanted was to be free of the heavy sacks. This was what they did to the rookies, they would get hazed until there was another new batch of recruits.

He was fine with it but, he wanted to get done and get back to the base. His feet were sore, his back was aching, and his teeth hurt, for some weird reason. No one told him when he signed up he'd been standing so much. If he wanted to do that, he would have taken a job like the dumb redneck in front of him.

"Put your stuff up here, boys," Gerry said, trying to sound cordial.

Roger glared at him. Maybe a bullet in his leg would do the redneck some good. Teach him some manners.

Peter put the mail bags up on the counter, seeing how Angry Roger was. Roger could get so wired sometimes. He needed to relax.

As both Army men raised their bags, they revealed their side-arms at their hips.

Dummy, attracted by the fresh meat, turned and looked. His dead eyes riveted in on the guns.

Guns.

More flashes went through his brain. Jennifer, running for her life. Blood running down his face. Army men. Jennifer was gray, cold, hungry. She bit one of them. They shot her. Rage and anger. Things he couldn't explain roared through him.

They'd killed Jennifer.

His Jennifer.

"What the hell is he staring at?" Roger glowered, pointing at Dummy. He hated zombies. He hated them even more when they stared at him like that.

"Who?" Gerry asked, turning around. He smacked Dummy upside the head with one of the letters.

Dummy staggered back. Jennifer, he thought. Who was Jennifer?

Yellow goes to yellow. Red goes to red.

"He's still staring at me," Roger said and pulled his gun.

"Hey!" Peter yelled. "Hold on, Roger, calm down!"

"Aw, hell," Gerry grumbled. He backed away. He wasn't about to get shot over some stupid zombie.

Dummy kept staring. He saw the gun again. Saw Jennifer getting shot. Saw the Army men turn their pistols on him. He felt pain, searing pain, worse than the Shockers. He remembered. They'd killed his Jennifer and then had killed him.

"Look at him, Peter!" Roger yelled. He was poking his gun at Dummy like it was a finger. The muzzle of the weapon was inches from Dummy's face. They were only separated by a counter. "He keeps staring at me. It ain't natural!"

Peter put his hand on Roger's arm. He had to calm the fool down. They couldn't go out to deliver the mail and end up shooting the post office up. How would that look?

"Take it easy," Peter said calmly.

Dummy leaned forward.

Gerry stepped away. He forgot all about the Shocker in his pocket. If he'd remembered and used it, maybe everything that followed wouldn't have happened. Maybe.

Roger stuck the gun up against Dummy's forehead. "I'm gonna do it!" he screamed.

"Hold it!" Travis yelled, trundling around the corner and down the hallway. He'd been in his office, enjoying a nice cup of coffee, when he heard all the yelling. What were people doing yelling in a post office?

When he saw the soldier pointing a gun on Dummy, his heart nearly exploded in his chest.

"Step away from that zombie!" Travis hollered. "He's Government property!"

Roger turned and looked at Travis, wondering who the pip-squeak was doing all the yelling.

It was all the opening Dummy needed. He swung his hand, slapping Roger, stunning the young man. With his other hand he moved, slowly, and snatched at the gun, knocking it to the side. Roger, panicking, squeezed the trigger.

The gun fired.

Fiery agony burned through Peter's stomach. He had just enough time to mutter the words, "What the hell?" before his legs gave out and he tumbled to the floor. Everything went black for a moment and then it all snapped back into focus. He was lying on his back, looking up at the ceiling, the blood rushing in his ears, drowning out the sounds of people yelling around him.

"The Shocker!" Travis screamed at Gerry. "Use the damn Shocker!"

Dummy tugged at the gun. This time, Roger got enough control to pump a couple of slugs into Dummy's chest. But of course, only a head shot would do anything to a zombie. Dummy still struggled while Gerry fumbled in his pants to grab the Shocker, not finding it.

Roger pulled away, the gun firing again. This bullet struck the counter and ricocheted up and to the side.

"The Shock…" Travis yelled, his voice suddenly cut off. That wasn't all. He was gagging on something, choking on hot blood bubbling in his mouth. His hands flew to his throat and came away covered in blood. He blinked, not comprehending what was happening. He sagged to the floor, gasping.

Gerry found the Shocker. It was too late, but he'd found it. He pressed the button, twice. All the zombies in the area pitched forward, moaning. All but Dummy.

He felt the pain. For sure, he felt the pain, but his little girl's face hovered in his vision. Jennifer giggling on the swing, her pigtails waving in the wind. His own laughter, disembodied. Her pigtails flying again, only this time splashing with blood, her blood. The Army men laughing at her. Laughing at him.

Dummy's hand clawed Roger's face. Roger screamed and dropped the gun. It fired one last time. The bullet hit the front of the counter and lodged there, harming no one. Dummy kept scraping, the ends of his clipped-off fingers finding soft spots. Tearing, rending.

Roger's bottom lip came off first in a long, agonizing rip. Dummy kept pulling down, peeling the skin off the soldier's face, revealing the glistening bone of Roger's chin. His other hand bore into Roger's eyes, scrabbling, churning, turning the gristle of the eyeballs into mush.

Gerry kept pressing the Shocker. The other zombies were on their backs now, shaking and quivering with the agony lancing through their brains. Gerry couldn't understand how Dummy was resisting like he was, how the stupid bag of pus was still ripping at the Army boy, pulling the kid's face off now. Blood was everywhere. Everywhere. Finally, he gave up, shoving the Shocker back into his pocket.

"Screw this," Gerry said, scrambling to the end of the counter. "I'm outta here."

He lifted the part of the counter that was on hinges, bringing it up just tall enough for him to slip under. He was going to run down the hall and call for help. Let the Army deal with this mess.

Unfortunately for him, Peter had just enough time to die and come back to life. He sat up, blood still leaking from his wound. He was hungry. He didn't understand much that was going on except he was confused and his stomach was screaming at him. He turned his head and spotted Gerry. The redneck looked good enough to eat.

Gerry stepped by Peter just as the newly risen zombie leaned forward and buried his teeth into Gerry's skin.

Gerry screamed. He looked down to see Peter yank out a bloody chunk of his thigh and gobble it down, torn jeans and all. He dug in his pocket again, pulling out the Shocker. He pointed it at Peter and pressed the button twice. Nothing happened, of course, because Peter wasn't outfitted for it to happen. Gerry's tiny moment of stupidity gave Peter the opportunity to bury his face in Gerry's testicles, getting a good mouthful.

Roger wasn't thinking about much anymore. Nothing but laying his head down and sleeping. But how could he sleep? He was bleeding so much. It was dark now, though, all the better to catch some rest. His mind didn't understand it was so dark because his eyes were gone, but that was okay. In a few minutes, he wouldn't care about anything other than eating. And as he slumped to the ground, he heard someone munching. He thought it sounded good.

Dummy stuck the bits of bloody flesh into his mouth. He'd forgotten how good it felt having the warm, slimy meat slither down his throat. He moaned with pleasure. This was it. This was all he cared about. All other thoughts fled his mind. He was nothing but bliss and happiness now.

Travis sat up, now one of the living dead. Much like Peter, he was hungrier than he'd ever thought possible. He saw Gerry, screaming and falling back against the counter, his pants torn open, blood gushing from his ruptured groin. Gerry would taste good, he thought. Travis reached out and snagged Gerry's remaining testicle dangling from the bite wound, swinging back and forth like the pendulum of a clock, still attached by the thinnest string of flesh. He wolfed it down. Never had anything tasted so good.

When Travis ate his right nut, Gerry gave up. There was no kind of life he wanted to live without his pecker and balls. He sank to the floor and let the two zombies eat away. Blood gurgled in his throat as he thought, 'Well, I had a hell of a run.'

Gerry, his cigarette still stuck to his bottom lip and smoldering as it burned out, closed his eyes and let go.

That was how the Second Great Rising began, in a small post office in Monkey's Paw, Kentucky. Peter, Travis, Roger, and Gerry ventured out from the lobby and into the rest of the building, killing the other few humans at work there. Once they were done, they left the post office, accompanied by their recently risen victims, and went out into the world.

People fell like dominos. The events in Monkey's Paw were just one rock thrown in a very large pond, but the ripples filtered out and affected everywhere.

Meanwhile, Dummy was back at work, putting envelopes away.

Yellow goes to yellow. Red goes to red. Over and over again.

ABOUT THE WRITERS

P. A. Douglas is a nationally touring singer-song writer, and author living in Texas. His debut novel "The End: A Zombie Novel" was published in 2011 by Living dead Press. To hear music and learn more about the author, visit www.indie-inside.com

Anthony Giangregorio is the author of 35 novels, almost all of them about zombies and has edited over 20 anthologies.

His work has appeared in Dead Science by Coscomentertainment, Dead Worlds: Undead Stories Volumes 1-7, and Wolves of War by Library of the Living Dead Press. He also has stories in End of Days: An Apocalyptic Anthology Vol. 1-5, the Book of the Dead series Vol. 1-6 by LDP, Zombie Zoology by Severed Press, and two anthologies with Pill Hill Press.

He is also the creator of the popular action/zombie series titled Deadwater and his action/ horror novel Dead Rage is being optioned for a movie. Check out his website at www.undeadpress.com.

Dane T. Hatchell lives in Baton Rouge, LA. He has stories appearing in over fifteen different anthologies from Living Dead Press. You can contact Dane at Enadious@gmail.com.

Kelly M. Hudson was born in Kentucky and currently resides in California. He loves horror and has over a dozen stories published in various anthologies, as well as a novel called The Turning published by Living Dead Press and available on Amazon.com and other places. If you wish to know more about Kelly, please visit his website www.kellymhudson.com for links to other stories and news.

Kelly M. Hudson was raised in Kentucky and lives in California. He loves him some zombies. He has two novels available through Living Dead Press: The Turning, a zombie novel, and Men of Perdition, a supernatural thriller. You can check out his website at www.kellymhudson.com for more info.

Matt Kurtz writes twisted tales for fun when not working at a small advertising company somewhere within the big state of Texas. His fiction can be found in anthologies from Pill Hill Press, Blood Bound Books, Comet Press and Necrotic Tissue Magazine.

Patrick MacAdoo is an author of supernatural thrillers. He currently lives in Portland, Oregon. His influences include Stephen King, Elmore Leonard, Shakespeare, Plato, and David Milch. He is currently seeking a publisher for his novel, "Big Box Byzantine." You can find Patrick on Facebook and email him at aspergo321@aol.com

Darren WJ Mills was born and raised in the county of Hertfordshire in the UK and to this day only lives a few miles away from his childhood home. Darren has had many jobs over the years including being an apprentice bricklayer, car salesman, production planner, recruitment consultant and he even studied to be a fitness trainer, but his dream has always been to be a horror writer, which was something he was determined to put time and effort into achieving after being made redundant from his previous job.

His love of horror, together with his humor and often joked about varying life experience, is something he hopes to bring to life within his written work.

Rick Moore's stories have appeared in numerous anthologies, including 'The Undead: Flesh Feast', 'History is Dead' and 'Cthulhu Unbound' (Permuted Press), the Stoker Award nominated 'Horror Library 3' (Cutting Block Press), 'The Beast Within' and Harvest Hill (Graveside Tales), 'Embark to Madness' (Coscom), 'Bound for Evil' (Dead Letter Press), and in several anthologies from Living Dead Press. Recently Rick joined Dark Moon Digest as an associate editor. His story 'Kindread' appeared in the third issue of the magazine.

Originally from England, he now lives in Phoenix, with his wife Ruth and three cats.

Go to http://www.myspace.com/zombieinfection for updates on published works and to contact the author.

J. L. Petty is an author of several short stories. She published her first book "Death and the Journalist" with Solstice Publishing, February 14, 2011. Her stories range in contemporary horror, suspense, science fiction, and fantasy fiction. Petty discovered her love of writing at an early age and started working as a contributor for The Virginian Pilot Newspaper. After working with the local newspaper in her hometown, she embarked upon a career in entertainment journalism. She's currently working towards a Masters degree and resides in Virginia.

Suzanne Robb has stories in current and upcoming anthologies with Coscom Entertainment, Pill Hill Press, Wicked East Press, Rhymefire, eBooks, Static Movement, Library of the Living Dead Press, Living Dead Press, Library of Fantasy, Norgus Press, Panic Press, and hidden Thoughts Press. She is also a member of Collaboration of the Dead. In her free time she reads, watches movies, plays with her dog, and enjoys chocolate and Legos. For more, check out Ramblings of an Anxiety Ridden Mind at http://suzannerobb.blogspot.com/

Katie Simmons resides in Canonsburg, Pennsylvania just outside of Pittsburgh. She has a long lived passion for writing, and the old west is her main interest where most of her stories take place. This is her first horror piece and her first piece of published work.

Rebecca Snow has been published in anthologies from Books of the Dead Press, May December Publications, Library of the Living Dead, Static Press, and Pill Hill Press. She and her husband herd cats in Virginia where the postman leaves complaining notes in their mailbox about dead things blocking the driveway. You can find her on Facebook (look for the bloody hand print) and Twitter @cemeteryflower.

PLANET OF THE DEAD
BOOK 1
by John Stowers

In the future, NASA's first yearlong mission to Mars mysteriously loses contact with Earth. When the desperate crew of the Space Shuttle Aldrin arrives home, there are no marching bands, fanfares, or joyous reunions to greet them, only a lonely trek across a barren world. At a darkened military base hidden in the desert, the crew stumbles upon a mystery of locked doors, disarray, and bloodstained walls. They also recover a dormant laptop, complete with a journal telling of a nightmarish pandemic sweeping across the planet.

Where society once rushed to and fro in the fast-paced and unceasing rat race of the early 21st century, the crew of the Aldrin now finds a world that shambles along on a crumbling highway, littered with desperate characters, flesh-craving zombies, and maybe, if they are lucky, a few living survivors.

Welcome to Earth.

Or by its new name, the *Planet of the Dead*.

AVAILABLE NOW! BOOK TWO OF PLANET OF THE DEAD: **SURVIVORS**

MONSTER PARTY
Edited by Anthony Giangregorio

Zombies, vampires, werewolves and ghosts are just a few of the monsters in this anthology.

But this isn't any anthology, you see, this is a party.

Or to be more to the point…a *Monster Party*.

Ever wonder what would happen if a werewolf and a zombie squared off? Or perhaps a vampire and a Frankenstein monster? Or better yet, how about a world where every conceivable monster is real and humans are their prey?

If those burning questions have been driving you mad, then look no further than this book.

So go on over to the buffet table, grab yourself a plate (the shrimp looks good) and get yourself a drink, and enjoy the fun ride that is the *Monster Party*.

THE WAR AGAINST THEM: A ZOMBIE NOVEL
by Jose Alfredo Vazquez

Mankind wasn't prepared for the onslaught.

An ancient organism is reanimating the dead bodies of its victims, creating worldwide chaos and panic as the disease spreads to every corner of the globe. As governments struggle to contain the disease, courageous individuals across the planet learn what it truly means to make choices as they struggle to survive.

Geopolitics meet technology in a race to save mankind from the worst threat it has ever faced. Doctors, military and soldiers from all walks of life battle to find a cure. For the dead walk, and if not stopped, they will wipe out all life on Earth. Humanity is fighting a war they cannot win, for who can overcome Death itself? Man versus the walking dead with the winner ruling the planet.

Welcome to *The War Against Them*.

NOVELLAS OF THE DEAD
STORIES OF A DEAD WORLD

Five tales of the walking dead await you if you dare to take the plunge. Travel to the future where the world is nothing but a ravaged wasteland, humans struggling to survive, each day a Hell on Earth. But sometimes, it's each other we need to fear the most. Then take a trip to the past, where the undead seek to rule the world of ancient Greece. Journey to Las Vegas, where a small group of travelers will find there are worse things than facing the living dead hunting them within a dilapidated casino. What would you do if the dead were banging at your door, trying to get in, and if they were fed the meat they craved, they would leave you alone, but there was nothing left to give them but your fellow companions? Would you commit murder and betrayal to save yourself? Would you become worse than the foe you were battling? In 1888, the dead won't remain in their coffins, and an intrepid doctor and a desperate father will battle the supernatural, all in the hopes of saving his family. When all is lost and mankind is at its darkest, the dead will rise to cover the land, feeding on all that is good and pure.

Can even man's indomitable will to survive be enough to stop the walking dead? Let's hope so.

DEAD HISTORY 2
A Zombie Anthology
Edited by Anthony Giangregorio

From the dawn of mankind, the walking dead have been with us.

The greatest moments in history are not what they appear.

Through the ages, the undead have been there, only the proof has been erased, documents destroyed, and witnesses silenced.

The living dead is man's greatest secret.

In this tome, are a few of the stories of what really happened all those years ago. History isn't alive, it's dead!

INSIDE THE PERIMETER: SCAVENGERS OF THE DEAD
by Alan Spencer

In the middle of nowhere, the vestiges of an abandoned town are surrounded by inescapably high concrete barriers, permitting no trespass or escape. The town is dormant of human life, but rampant with the living dead, who choose not to eat flesh, but to instead continue their survival by cruder means.

Boyd Broman, a detective arrested and falsely imprisoned, has been transferred into the secret town. He is given an ultimatum: recapture Hayden Grubaugh, the cannibal serial killer, who has been banished to the town, in exchange for his freedom.

During Boyd's search, he discovers why the psychotic cannibal must really be captured and the sinister secrets the dead town holds.

With no chance of escape, Broman finds himself trapped among the ravenous, violent dead. With the cannibal feeding on the animated cadavers and the undead searching for Boyd, he must fulfill his end of the deal before the rotting corpses turn him into an unwilling organ donor.

But Boyd wasn't told that no one gets out alive, that the town is a death sentence. For there is no escape from *Inside the Perimeter*.

DEAD RAGE

by Anthony Giangregorio
Book 2 in the Rage virus series!

An unknown virus spreads across the globe, turning ordinary people into bloodthirsty, ravenous killers.

Only a small percentage of the population is immune and soon become prey to the infected.

Amongst the infected comes a man, stricken by the virus, yet still retaining his grasp on reality. His need to destroy the *normals* becomes an obsession and he raises an army of killers to seek out and kill all who aren't *changed* like himself. A few survivors gather together on the outskirts of Chicago and find themselves running for their lives as the specter of death looms over all.

The Dead Rage virus will find you, no matter where you hide.

CHRISTMAS IS DEAD: A ZOMBIE ANTHOLOGY

Edited by Anthony Giangregorio

Twas the night before Christmas and all through the house, not a creature was stirring, not even a. . . zombie?

That's right; this anthology explores what would happen at Christmas time if there was a full blown zombie outbreak. Reanimated turkeys, zombie Santas, and demon reindeers that turn people into flesh-eating ghouls are just some of the tales you will find in this merry undead book. So curl up under the Christmas tree with a cup of hot chocolate, and as the fireplace crackles with warmth, get ready to have your heart filled with holiday cheer. But of course, then it will be ripped from your heaving chest and fed upon by blood-thirsty elves with a craving for human flesh! For you see, Christmas is Dead!

And you will never look at the holiday season the same way again.

BLOOD RAGE

(The Prequel to DEAD RAGE)

by Anthony Giangregorio

The madness descended before anyone knew what was happening. Perfectly normal people suddenly became rage-fueled killers, tearing and slicing their way across the city. Within hours, Chicago was a battlefield, the dead strewn in the streets like trash.

Stacy, Chad and a few others are just a few of the immune, unaffected by the virus but not to the violence surrounding them. The *changed* are ravenous, sweeping across Chicago and perhaps the world, destroying any *normals* they come across. Fire, slaughter, and blood rule the land, and the few survivors are now an endangered species.

This is the story of the first days of the Dead Rage virus and the brave souls who struggle to live just one more day.

When the smoke clears, and the *changed* have maimed and killed all who stand in their way, only the strong will remain.

The rest will be left to rot in the sun.

KINGDOM OF THE DEAD
by Anthony Giangregorio
THE DEAD HAVE RISEN!

In the dead city of Pittsburgh, two small enclaves struggle to survive, eking out an existence of hand to mouth.

But instead of working together, both groups battle for the last remaining fuel and supplies of a city filled with the living dead.

Six months after the initial outbreak, a lone helicopter arrives bearing two more survivors and a newborn baby. One enclave welcomes them, while the other schemes to steal their helicopter and escape the decaying city.

With no police, fire, or social services existing, the two will battle for dominance in the steel city of the walking dead. But when the dust settles, the question is: will the remaining humans be the winners, or the losers?

When the dead walk, the line between Heaven and Hell is so twisted and bent there is no line at all.

RISE OF THE DEAD
by Anthony Giangregorio
DEATH IS ONLY THE BEGINNING!

In less than forty-eight hours, more than half the globe was infected.

In another forty-eight, the rest would be enveloped.

The reason?

A science experiment gone horribly wrong which enabled the dead to walk, their flesh rotting on their bones even as they seek human prey.

Jeremy was an ordinary nineteen year old slacker. He partied too much and had done poorly in high school. After a night of drinking and drugs, he awoke to find the world a very different place from the one he'd left the night before.

The dead were walking and feeding on the living, and as Jeremy stepped out into a world gone mad, the dead spotting him alone and unarmed in the middle of the street,
he had to wonder if he would live long enough to see his twentieth birthday.

THE CHRONICLES OF JACK PRIMUS
BOOK ONE
by Michael D. Griffiths

Beneath the world of normalcy we all live in lies another world, one where supernatural beings exist. These creatures of the night hunt us; want to feed on our very souls, though only a few know of their existence.

One such man is Jack Primus, who accidentally pierces the veil between this world and the next. With no other choice if he wants to live, he finds himself on the run, hunted by beings called the Xemmoni, an ancient race that sees humans as nothing but cattle. They want his soul, to feed on his very essence, and they will kill all who stand in their way. But if they thought Jack would just lie down and accept his fate, they were sorely mistaken.   He didn't ask for this battle, but he knew he would fight them with everything at his disposal, for to lose is a fate worse than death.

He would win this war, and he would take down anyone who got in his way.

PLAYING GOD: A ZOMBIE NOVEL
by Jeffery Dye

It was supposed to be a regeneration virus to help soldiers on the battlefield—regrowing limbs and healing wounds— but a simple act of carelessness unleashed it on an unsuspecting world.

For the virus was not perfected, and once exposed, the host quickly dies, only to rise again as one of the undead.

As countries are quickly overrun, scientists and military teams battle to contain the outbreak.

There is no other option.

If the infection continues to spread, soon the entire globe will be consumed. And perhaps that will be a just punishment for a mankind that dared to try to play God.

DEAD HOUSE: A ZOMBIE GHOST STORY
by Keith Adam Luethke

The old mansion on the edge of town, aptly named Dead House, has a history of blood, pain, and death, but what Victor Leeds knows of this past only scratches the surface of the true horrors within.

But when his girlfriend is attacked by a shadowy figure one rainy night, he soon finds himself caught up in a world where the dead walk and ghostly wraiths abound. And to make matters worse, a pair of serial killers are fulfilling carefully made plans, and when they are done, the small town of Stormville, New York will run red. The last ingredient to open the gates of Hell, and plunge this small upstate town into madness, is rain.

And in Stormville, it pours by the gallons.

THE LAZARUS CULTURE
by Pasquale J. Morrone

Secret Service Agent Christopher Kearns had no idea what he was up against. Assigned on a temporary basis to the Center for Disease Control, he only knew that somehow it was connected to the lives of those the agency protected...namely, the President of the United States. If there were possible terrorist activities in the making, he could only guess it was at a red alert basis.

When Kearns meets and befriends Doctor Marlene Peterson of the Breezy Point Medical Center in Maryland, he soon finds that science fiction can indeed become a reality. In a solitary room walked a man with no vital signs: dead. The explanation he received came from Doctor Lee Fret, a man assigned to the case from the CDC. Something was attached to the brain stem. Something alive that was quickly spreading rapidly through Maryland and other states.

Kearns and his ragtag army of agents and medical personnel soon find themselves in a world of meaningless slaughter and mayhem. The armies of the walking dead were far more than mere zombies. Some began to change into whatever it was they ate. The government had found a way to reanimate the dead by implanting a parasite found on the tongue of the Red Snapper to the human brain. It looked good on paper, but it was a project straight from Hell. The dead now walked, but it wasn't a mystery. It was The Lazarus Culture.

THE DEAD OF SPACE: BRAVE NEW WORLD

by Jeremiah Coe

Welcome to the future of the walking dead! The Earth is freezing over. After a deep space probe returns with information of another habitable planet at the end of our galaxy, a desperate attempt to save mankind is implemented. The Intrepid, a massive starship with a crew of 500, is sent to investigate the world designated E-eleven-two for possible habitation of the human race. The world looks perfect, clear springs, tall mountains, open fields, even the remnants of the planet's native inhabitants still exist, right down to the structures they one lived in. And there are no native species to threaten the newly arrived human population. It's perfect...it's paradise. A mystery arrives in the form of the planet's previous inhabitant's corpses, found frozen under the polar ice caps, thousands of them, all perfectly preserved.

The scientists, in their excitement, hastily bring back fifty of the bodies to base camp, each one perfectly preserved and ready to be dissected and studied. As the bodies thaw out and await dissection, first one, then another begins to move, and soon, they start to walk; despite being dead for hundreds if not thousands of years The crew of the Intrepid are about to find out what happened to the natives of E-eleven-two, and are going to discover to their horror that they didn't die out naturally.

In fact, there was nothing natural about their demise.

The future isn't full of hope...the future is dead.

UNITED STATES OF ARMAGEDDON

by Jeffrey Thomas Crooms

THE END OF A COUNTRY!

America's enemies plot a sadistic plan to destroy the population and armed forces so they can swoop in and rule the country.

Terrorists called the Horsemen smuggle in a deadly biological weapon straight to the heart of the United States and release it.

The result is a land covered with corpses, bloated bodies strewn from sea to sea.

A few desperate survivors battle through the blighted landscape on a last ditch mission to save the country from total domination.

But the biological weapon has a side effect, one no one would have ever foreseen, one too unimaginable to even contemplate.

Welcome to the future. Welcome to the Unite States of _Armageddon_

BOOK OF THE DEAD

ISBN 978-1-935458-25-8

Edited by Anthony Giangregorio

This is the most faithful, truest zombie anthology ever written, and we invite you along for the ride. Every single story in this book is filled with slack-jawed, eyes glazed, slow moving, shambling zombies set in a world where the dead have risen and only want to eat the flesh of the living. In these pages, the rules are sacrosanct. There is no deviation from what a zombie should be or how they came about. The Dead Walk.

There is no reason, though rumors and suppositions fill the radio and television stations. But the only thing that is fact is that the walking dead are here and they will not go away. So prepare yourself for the ultimate homage to the master of zombie legend. And remember... Aim for the head!

THE BOOK OF CANNIBALS
ISBN 13: 978-1-935458-52-4   ISBN 10: 1-935458-52-3
ARE YOU HUNGRY YET?

THE UNNATURAL DEAD

A ZOMBIE NOVEL

DARREN WJ MILLS

CLAN OF THE BIGFOOT
ANTHONY GIANGREGORIO

www.ingramcontent.com/pod-product-compliance
Lightning Source LLC
Chambersburg PA
CBHW070949120726
47910CB00004B/1168